She owed him. Big-time.

A lot more than the glass of icy lemonade she was bringing him now. Intending to give him the drink, say her piece and leave, she called his name. But when he turned around, the only sound she uttered was a gasp.

Nick had removed his shirt as he put together the swing set, and for the first time she saw his muscles and his broad chest. In the midday sun his pecs and six-pack abs glistened like Cortez's gold. She stood there, her mouth agape, her mind blank. She'd wanted to tell him something, but couldn't remember what.

She closed her mouth and swallowed, snapping herself out of her trance. "Thanks for doing this, Nick."

He gave her that devastating smile. "No problem."

It was a problem, all right. Her girls loved Nick, so she had to risk spending a little time with him. But could she resist the temptation?

Dear Reader,

Welcome to my new three-book miniseries, DALLAS DUETS, about three young women who live in the same fourplex in Dallas.

The first story is about a woman who feels rather alone in the world—that is, until she reaches out to some young children who really need a change in their lives. I was inspired to write this story because of something I'd seen on television about The Heart Gallery, an organization that enlists the help of the world's top photographers to find homes for children who are up for adoption. You can find more information about them online.

I hope you enjoy this story as much as I enjoyed writing it. As always, I hope you appreciate my view about the importance of family, whether it's made up of people who are related by blood, or a family of your own making.

If you have any comments or questions, you can contact me at my Web site, www.judychristenberry.com.

Happy reading!

Judy Christenberry

Judy Christenberry
DADDY NEXT DOOR

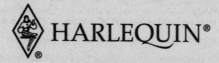

HARLEQUIN®

TORONTO • NEW YORK • LONDON
AMSTERDAM • PARIS • SYDNEY • HAMBURG
STOCKHOLM • ATHENS • TOKYO • MILAN • MADRID
PRAGUE • WARSAW • BUDAPEST • AUCKLAND

ISBN-13: 978-0-373-75149-5
ISBN-10:   0-373-75149-4

DADDY NEXT DOOR

ABOUT THE AUTHOR

Judy Christenberry has been writing romances for over fifteen years because she loves happy endings as much as her readers do. A former French teacher, Judy now devotes herself to writing full-time. She hopes readers have as much fun with her stories as she does. She spends her spare time reading, watching her favorite sports teams and keeping track of her two daughters. Judy lives in Texas.

Books by Judy Christenberry

HARLEQUIN AMERICAN ROMANCE

853—PATCHWORK FAMILY
867—RENT A MILLIONAIRE GROOM
878—STRUCK BY THE TEXAS MATCHMAKERS†
885—RANDALL PRIDE*
901—TRIPLET SECRET BABIES
918—RANDALL RICHES*
930—RANDALL HONOR*
950—RANDALL WEDDING*
969—SAVED BY A TEXAS-SIZED WEDDING†
1000—A RANDALL RETURNS*
1033—REBECCA'S LITTLE SECRET**
1058—RACHEL'S COWBOY**
1073—A SOLDIER'S RETURN**
1097—A TEXAS FAMILY REUNION**
1117—VANESSA'S MATCH**
1133—A RANDALL THANKSGIVING

*Brides for Brothers
†Tots for Texans
**Children of Texas

Chapter One

A suitcase in each hand, Nick Barry shoved open the front door to the fourplex on Yellow Rose Lane. The residential North Dallas neighborhood was exactly what he needed. A tree-lined street, freshly mowed grass and peace and quiet.

No wonder his aunt had loved this place. Too bad she had to leave it, he thought, but at least she'd sublet it to him. Between the low rent and the amenities, it was a sweet deal.

He was in the lobby, having used the key Aunt Grace had sent to get in the front door. Now he was trying to figure out which key unlocked his new apartment when he heard someone behind him. He looked over his shoulder but not seeing anyone, he turned back to his task.

Simultaneously he felt something around his ankle and heard a tiny voice yelling, "I found him! I found our daddy!"

Shock filled him as he stared at the little girl sitting on the floor with her short, thin arms wrapped around his left leg.

He'd been a little forgetful lately, what with the change in his life, but he was pretty sure he hadn't forgotten a child.

"Missy? Missy, where are you?" This time it wasn't a child's voice, but a woman's. And if the woman herself matched her tone, she was a beauty. The sound came from afar so he decided to encourage her to come closer.

"Um, I think Missy is with me in the entry hall," he yelled. He looked down at the towheaded preschooler staring up at him. "You are Missy, aren't you?"

She nodded brightly, not appearing at all scared.

"Missy?"

The woman was getting closer, but Nick called again. "She's here with me in the lobby!"

When the door across from his aunt's apartment swung open, Nick knew he'd been right: the flesh and blood woman matched her voice. The blond beauty rushed out. "Missy! I told you not to come out here without me! Get back inside at once."

"But I found him!" Missy said indignantly, hugging his leg even tighter.

"Who did you find?" the blonde demanded.

Nick was finding the situation amusing until two other little girls appeared behind the adult. He'd forgotten *three* daughters? "Uh, I don't think—"

"Missy, let go of—of whoever you are!" The blonde looked at him for the first time.

"Nick Barry."

"Okay. Missy, let go of Nick Barry. He is not your daddy!"

"Whew! That's a relief," Nick said, grinning.

"This is not a laughing matter!" the young woman said sternly.

"Why can't he be our daddy?" Missy asked, still not letting him go.

"Because I don't even know who he is!"

"But we need a daddy!" Missy protested, her tone getting more indignant.

Nick looked down at the charmer hanging on to his ankle. He set down the two suitcases he'd been carrying and then bent down and picked her up. "Sweetheart, I'm sure wherever your daddy is, he'll come soon. I can't believe he'd ever forget you."

Suddenly one of the older girls burst into tears and, sobbing, ran back into the apartment across from him.

"Was it something I said?" Nick asked, frowning.

The woman stepped forward and took Missy into her arms. "Why are you here?" she asked him, looking around. "And how did you get in?"

Ah. She'd finally started asking important questions. "I'm subletting this apartment."

"Grace's apartment? She can only sublet it to a relative and what happened to her? The last time I saw her she was doing fine!"

"She's moved into an assisted-living facility. And I'm her nephew."

"Okay, fine. I'll deal with you later. Now I have to—"

"Jennifer, the stove is exploding!" another young voice called out from inside the woman's apartment.

"What? Get out of the kitchen! I'm coming!"

Seemingly without thinking, she set Missy down and ran back into the apartment, frantic.

Missy grinned up at him. "Won't you be our daddy?"

"Uh, no, but I will see if I can help your mommy. Come on." He scooped up the little girl and entered the apartment. Missy showed him the way to the kitchen.

The blonde was on her way out of the room. "What are you doing in here?"

"You forgot something." He nodded toward the child in his arms.

"Just put her down. I've got to see about Steffi!" Then, like a whirlwind, she moved on to another room.

"Who is Steffi?" he asked Missy once he'd set her on her feet.

"She's my big sister," Missy said solemnly. "You made her cry."

"I did? How did I do that?"

Missy's big brown eyes sobered. "She remembers our real daddy. And he's dead."

"Oh, I'm sorry."

"What's dead mean?"

Nick stared at the precocious child. "Um, I think you need to ask your mommy."

"She's dead, too." The little girl was beginning to tear up and Nick felt his heart breaking for her and her sisters. He tried to think of something to distract her.

"What was exploding in the kitchen?" he asked.

"I don't know. Jennifer was making sketti for us."

"Sketti? What's that?"

"You know, long, skinny things with red stuff on it. It's my favorite!"

With Missy's description and from what he could see in the kitchen, he figured out their mother was making them spaghetti. The stove was turned off under the big pan of water and pasta. Nick was an expert on spaghetti, by virtue of the hundreds of pounds he'd eaten just in his adult life. He checked the spaghetti and determined it still needed to cook awhile. The sauce, in a smaller pot, was already getting cold. He put Missy in a chair at a nearby table and told her not to get down.

"Why?"

"Because I don't want you to get burned."

"Oh." The little girl seemed satisfied with that logic.

He turned on the burners and stirred the sauce as he watched the water begin to boil.

"I didn't know daddies could cook," Missy commented from the table.

"Some daddies can," he muttered, concentrating on what he was doing.

"Jennifer says we don't need no daddy."

"Who is Jennifer?" he asked, expecting to be told Jennifer was one of her sisters.

"She's our new mommy," Missy said with satisfaction.

"Your *new* mommy?"

"Yes. She's our new mommy today."

"You've only lived with her today?"

"Yes. Steffi said she skewed us," Missy said carefully.

"She skewed you? I don't understand what that means."

"You know, like when Superman skews a baby. He saves her."

Ah, *rescue,* he reasoned. But how had Jennifer rescued these precious children? Treading carefully so as not to bring a second child to tears, he decided to back into his questions.

"So you watch Superman?" he asked.

"Yes, my last mommy played it on the television a lot. Superman skewed somebody every time—"

"So you're saying your new mommy rescued you?" he asked, sparing Missy a glance.

"Yeah, that's what Steffi said."

He stirred the sauce as he watched the spaghetti boil. When he checked the spaghetti again, it appeared to be ready. He found a metal colander sitting in the sink, ready for him to pour the spaghetti and boiling water in it, so he did so. Steam rose in the air.

"Is that smoke?" Missy asked casually. "Jennifer says smoke is dangerous."

"No, it's steam. That's a little different, but it can also hurt you if you're not careful." He wondered what he should do now.

Hearing a noise in the hallway, he turned in that direction. The blonde reappeared in the doorway. The adult blonde, that is. Jennifer. All three little girls were also blond. But then he'd originally thought Jennifer was their birth mother. Not according to Missy.

"Why are you still here?" Her demand wasn't exactly welcoming, but he realized she was under a little stress.

"I thought I could lend a hand. Especially since it appears I caused part of the problem."

"Part?" she said, giving him a direct look.

For the first time he noticed she had gorgeous blue eyes to go with the blond hair.

"I didn't volunteer to be anyone's daddy by just coming in the door, did I?"

"I guess not," she said, not sounding happy about having to admit it.

"How's Steffi?" he asked, afraid she was about to tell him to leave. He was strangely reluctant to do so.

Steffi peeked at him from behind her new mommy.

"She's fine."

"I'm glad. I didn't mean to upset you," he said to the little girl.

She nodded, then hid behind the woman.

"Well, the spaghetti is ready, and the sauce, too. And, hey, you've got hamburger meat in your sauce, you lucky girls!" he joked. During college, he hadn't been able to afford meat for his spaghetti.

"You finished cooking it?" Jennifer asked in consternation. "I didn't intend— That's very kind of you. Uh, would you like to join us?"

Missy perked up at that invitation. "Yeah! You can have the daddy seat!"

"Missy, no, Mr. Barry is not the daddy. He's a guest. We'll welcome him to his new apartment and thank him for his assistance. Well?" she asked, looking at him again.

"Only if you'll promise to call me Nick. I don't like formality."

She took a deep breath and he feared she was going to refuse, leaving him no option but to decline her invitation. And he didn't want to do that.

"Of course, Nick. Steffi, can you and Annie get everyone a knife, fork and spoon?"

"Yes, Jennifer," the oldest girl said.

"Is there anything I can do?" Nick asked.

"No, we'll manage. You can entertain Missy."

Nick grinned. He'd already entertained the little girl, but he settled in at the table beside her. "Looks like it's you and me, Missy."

"You and me what?"

"You and me who don't have a job. We just get to watch."

"Oh, yeah. I'm too little. But you're old. How come you don't have a job?"

Nick stifled a laugh. "Because I'm your guest."

"Oh." Missy rested her chin on her hands and seemed deep in thought.

"Is iced tea okay, Nick?" his hostess asked.

"Yes, that'll be fine. Uh, Missy said your name is Jennifer?"

"Yes, I'm sorry, I forgot to introduce myself. I'm Jennifer Carpenter, and these are my three daughters, Steffi, Annie and Missy, whom I believe you met earlier."

"Definitely. Hello, girls. You sure look like your mother." Okay, so he was fishing for information. He'd admit he was curious.

Steffi looked at him and calmly said, "Thank you." Despite her earlier emotions she was now composed.

"Are you eight years old, Steffi?" he asked. He was pretty good at guessing the ages of children, since he'd been a schoolteacher and had several nieces and nephews.

"No, I'm only six."

"Well, you seem much older." From her slight smile she appeared pleased. "How about you, Annie?" he asked gently, realizing the middle child was much shyer than her older sister.

She stared at him, not saying anything.

Steffi spoke for her sister. "She's five and Missy is three."

He took another look at his hostess. She certainly didn't look like the mother of three children. Her slender form, including a very flat stomach, would've fooled most anyone.

"You have a beautiful family, Jennifer."

After sending the girls a special smile, she looked at him and said, "Thank you."

She carried a platter of spaghetti covered in meat sauce, topped by grated cheese.

"You use cheddar cheese on your spaghetti?" he asked in surprise.

"Yes. The girls like it."

Her voice was cool and he hurriedly said, "I'm sure I will, too."

Since she added a tossed salad and warm garlic bread, he had no complaints.

As much as he tried to make conversation, there wasn't much talking during dinner, nor the noise he expected with three young children. When they needed it, Jennifer corrected their table manners, but she was gentle and didn't embarrass the girls. Despite the quiet, Nick couldn't have enjoyed the meal more—unless of course Jennifer actually spoke to him. Still, he enjoyed stealing glances at her soft honey-colored hair and expressive blue eyes. He had time to find out her story, after dinner.

As soon as the girls were finished, Jennifer stood and said, "Thank you for joining us, Nick. We hope you like your apartment." The polite version of "Here's your hat. What's your hurry?"

Deliberately he stayed put. "I'm sure I will. Do you know the owners?"

"Yes," she said with some hesitancy, which made him even more curious about her.

"Do you think I need to contact them? Aunt Grace wasn't clear about that."

"No, the lease says she can sublet to a relative, so there isn't anything the owner can do." Diverting her gaze, she started to clean the table.

He stood up immediately. "Let me help you with that."

She put a hand out to stop him, but when it landed on his arm, she yanked it back. "N-no thank you. I'll clean up later, after I give the girls their baths and tuck them into bed."

"I could do it while you take care of the kids."

"No!" Then, apparently realizing the vehemence in her tone, she sidestepped him and regained her poise. "A guest never does the dishes, Mr. Barry."

"Well, in that case, Ms. Carpenter, thank you." As much as he didn't want to, he walked to the door, his hostess behind him. When he reached the hall, she stepped out, too.

"Oh, look. I forgot you dropped your suitcases out here. I'm sorry."

"Doesn't look like a problem. Don't you worry."

"Well, then, good night." She turned and walked back into her apartment, but something made him stop her. For some reason he felt an overwhelming urge to get to know Ms. Jennifer Carpenter. He reached out and grabbed the door before she could close it.

"I…wanted to ask you…" He searched for some innocuous question to prolong the evening. "Are the other renters nice?" How glib, old man. With lines like that you'll dazzle her with your wit.

"Very nice. In fact, your upstairs neighbors will welcome you most heartily. They're six flight attendants."

He let his eyes slowly appreciate her face. She was a beauty, with soft, wavy blond hair that shone like the sun, and flawless skin. With a neighbor like this, he wasn't sure the women upstairs could even compete. But she was obviously sending a message: *Look elsewhere for your entertainment.*

He had no choice but to comply. For now.

RIGHT NOW. SHE NEEDED TO get Mr. Nick Barry out of her mind right now. Her new neighbor had no business occupying her thoughts when she was in soapsuds up to her elbows and watching three little girls in the bathtub. Her attention had to be totally focused on her children.

But it was difficult. Not the bathing. The thinking. Every time she reined in her errant thoughts, they found a way back to Nick.

Truth to tell, the man was charming. Handsome. Great with the girls.

Not now, Jennifer! Now was the time she'd waited for, wanted so desperately. Her with Steffi, Annie and Missy.

One by one she took them out of the tub and helped them dry. "Did everyone get a clean nightgown and panties?"

Missy slapped a hand over her mouth. "I forgot!"

"Missy!" Steffi complained.

"It's all right, Steffi. Come with me, Missy, and I'll help you." She'd carefully showed the girls where she'd put their new clothes earlier that afternoon.

She'd found out three days ago that she'd been approved as the girls' foster mother while she waited for the court to approve her application for adoption.

As soon as she'd gotten work, she'd bought them each a couple of outfits and underwear and nightgowns to wear until they made a real shopping trip.

Missy clutched the clean clothes to her chest as they walked back to the bath. "Do I get to keep these?"

"Yes, of course, sweetie."

"And I don't got to share them?"

"No, Missy, these are for you all by yourself."

"Good."

She was learning a lot about children in foster homes. Missy and Steffi had regaled her with stories, many of which nearly broke her heart. Annie, on the other hand, didn't say much, but she was the reason Jennifer had requested to foster the three little sisters until the adoption went through.

And probably the reason her request had been granted.

That and her uncle—a judge in the Dallas juvenile courts.

"Are you going to take more pictures of us?" Missy asked as they reached the bathroom.

"Of course I will. But not tonight."

"Oh. Okay."

"It's too late for pictures tonight. You need to get in bed so you'll get enough sleep to grow."

Missy immediately stretched up as high as she could reach. "I'm going to grow *this* big!" she exclaimed.

"No, you're not, Missy! Stop exaggerating," Steffi said, always the big sister.

Jennifer chuckled. "Actually, Steffi, she probably will. Just not tonight." She turned on the faucet. "Brush your teeth, girls. I bought each of you a new toothbrush."

"Really?" Missy asked in awe. "A new nightgown *and* a new toothbrush?"

"Yes, Missy," Jennifer said, laughing again.

She made sure Missy knew how to brush her teeth and helped the other two. Then after the girls dressed for bed, Jennifer led them to their room. She'd originally thought about giving the eldest child, Steffi, a separate room, since there were three bedrooms. But she changed her mind and bought a shiny red bed that was full on bottom and twin on top. That would allow all three sisters to be together.

For them, it was something new.

"I love our new bed, Jennifer," Steffi told her as she tucked them in.

"I'm glad, sweetheart. I wanted you to have something that you'd like. And red makes me smile."

"Me, too. And I like living here with you and my sisters."

Jennifer bent over and kissed Steffi's cheek. "I love it, too, honey. We're going to be happy together."

"Me, too!" Missy called. "Will we get to see our daddy tomorrow?"

Jennifer sighed. Why did Missy have to remind her of Nick? "That man is not your daddy, sweetie. We don't have a daddy here. It's just us girls."

"Yeah" came softly from Annie.

Jennifer ducked down and kissed Missy's cheek, too. Annie was on the far side, but Jennifer reached over to kiss her also.

"Good night, Annie. Sleep tight."

The little girl stared at her with big brown eyes, a solemn look on her face. A look too old for a five year old.

Jennifer gave her a smile and then tiptoed to the door, turning out the light.

"See, the night-light keeps the room from getting dark. Is everyone okay with that?"

Missy and Steffi assured her they were fine with the night-light. Annie said nothing.

"Good night," Jennifer called one last time before she walked quietly down the hall.

After she cleaned up and made herself a cup of instant decaf coffee, she sat down and sighed. She'd made it through the first day of her new life.

She'd picked up the three sisters this morning at ten o'clock and brought them back to her house after three days of frantic planning and shopping.

But the change had been set in motion three weeks ago, when she'd volunteered, as a professional photographer, to take photos of foster children. The program was called the Heart Gallery and was taking place all over the country. These professional, quality photos replaced the horrible mug shots that had been all potential families had to look at.

It had seemed a more than worthwhile project to Jennifer. When she'd drawn three sisters to photograph, she'd been enchanted to find such beautiful children as her subjects. She planned to spend the day with them, photographing them, treating them to lunch, making a good memory for them. Since she and her mother were estranged, she thought it might make a nice memory for her, too.

Jennifer admired the bond between the sisters, even envied it. She herself had no siblings, except for a half brother whom she'd met only once. Her father, after divorcing her mother, had no intention of ever having anything to do with Jennifer or her mother. But since his death, she had thought about contacting her half brother. Spending the day with the three little girls convinced her. Jennifer's heart broke when she recalled the photo shoot. Two of the three children smiled broadly, their personalities coming through the camera lens. It was the middle child Jennifer had trouble capturing. She'd coaxed and cajoled Annie, even taken the five-year-old in her arms. But Annie pulled away, as if in pain. That was when Jennifer discovered the bruises all over Annie's body.

The child wouldn't tell her how she'd gotten her

bruises. Steffi finally said that the "bad man" who lived in the foster house did that to her if she didn't obey him fast enough.

Jennifer had called Child Protective Services and demanded that the girls' welfare worker come at once. Six hours later, the overworked welfare worker arrived at her door. When Jennifer showed the woman the bruises all over Annie's body and demanded the child be removed from her home at once, the worker had said she had nowhere to put her.

Without hesitation Jennifer had offered to take her. On a temporary basis, of course.

The welfare worker said she would have to be approved and that could take weeks. That was when Jennifer had called her uncle and demanded he do something.

With his help she was allowed to keep all three girls overnight, and the next morning she received approval to keep Annie. But by then she'd seen the love and need the three girls had for one another, and though it meant a huge change in her own life, she'd asked for custody of all three.

And today her new life had begun.

Only to be interrupted by her new neighbor, Missy's "daddy."

Chapter Two

The new apartment felt like home fairly quickly.

He'd unpacked his two suitcases in record time and had put his toiletries in the bathroom. Aunt Grace's personal items had been removed, so settling in was easy enough.

He smiled warmly when he thought of his aunt. He had such fond memories of the elderly woman. Though she hadn't wanted to leave Yellow Rose Lane, she was simply unable to live by herself any longer. The assisted-living facility was close by, so Nick could visit her often.

Meantime she'd offered him the apartment for the remaining eleven months of her lease. It was all the time he needed. Grace had called the fourplex home for ten years, and her rent had never been raised the entire time, making his payment much less than what he was shelling out every month for a small place in Lubbock. He felt a little bad about taking advantage of the owners, but he didn't know them. Aunt Grace had told him to talk to her neighbor across the hall.

Jennifer.

Truthfully, he'd like to do more than just talk to the pretty blonde. But yesterday's meeting hadn't gone too well.

He fought the urge to go back to her apartment. He had things to do—like go to a grocery store and lay in some food. That was what a responsible man would do. He wouldn't interrupt the beauty across the hall just because of his curiosity. That was the reason he gave himself.

Of course, he wouldn't.

But when he opened his door, he didn't go out to his car. He crossed the hall and knocked on her door.

He heard the sound of little feet running and Jennifer's voice cautioning Missy not to open the door.

When the door opened, it was Jennifer, not Missy, who stared at him.

"Yes?"

"I'm sorry to bother you. I need to go buy groceries, and I wondered if you could tell me where the closest grocery store is."

"Yes. There are two close by." She began giving him directions, and he sent her a bewildered look.

"I'm afraid I don't know the roads around here. Could you draw me a map?" he asked politely. Then he noticed little Missy peeking around the door. "Hi, there."

The giggle he received in response brought a smile to his lips.

Jennifer didn't appear amused at his greeting. "Missy, go back and finish your breakfast."

Little fingers curled in a wave and Missy ran back down the hall.

With a sigh, Jennifer said, "Come in and I'll draw a map."

"I really appreciate it," he assured her. As he followed her into the kitchen, he sniffed the elixir he needed each morning.

"You made coffee? I mean, uh, what kind of coffee do you buy? It smells good."

Another sigh. Okay, he hadn't been subtle, but he hadn't expected to smell coffee.

"Would you like a cup?" she offered.

"I'd kill for one," he admitted in a low voice. Somehow, saying that even jokingly in front of such innocent ears didn't seem right.

"Have a seat," she said, gesturing to the breakfast table where the three girls were eating.

He joined them, trying not to look at the pancakes they were eating. He should've found a grocery store last night, but his stomach had been full. And he'd been tired.

Jennifer brought him a cup of steaming hot coffee. "Bless you," he said.

She gave him a knowing look and turned away.

He closed his eyes as he sipped wonderful coffee. Without a doubt, he needed to know what brand she used. When he opened his eyes to ask that important question, he saw that she was occupied at the stove again.

She turned around and put a plate of pancakes in front of him. Then she got him a knife and fork. "Butter and syrup are on the table."

"I didn't mean— You didn't have to cook for me!" he exclaimed, feeling embarrassed.

"I was cooking for the girls, anyway. Eat them, don't eat them. Your choice."

He immediately reached for the butter and syrup. "I won't turn them down."

She was still at the stove and he realized she'd given him the pancakes she would've eaten. "Hey, let me cook those and you come eat."

"No, I'm fine. Don't let those get cold."

He spread butter over his pancakes and added syrup. Then he took his first bite. "Wow, these are great, aren't they, girls?"

Three little heads bobbed up and down.

"They just gave you a rave review, Jennifer, but their mouths were full. You couldn't hear them," he said, smiling at the kids.

"I know. They already told me." She dished up her pancakes and joined them at the table. "This is a special breakfast today."

"Ah, first breakfast since school got out?"

"Nice try, but I know Missy told you I was their *new* mommy. Did you think I kidnapped them?"

He smiled at her. She looked beautiful, dressed in

Bermuda shorts and a knit shirt. "If all kidnappers looked like you, no victims would ever complain."

She glared at him.

"Just teasing. No, I didn't think you kidnapped them. I figured I'd find out eventually what was going on."

She took a bite of her pancakes and chewed slowly.

Nick said nothing else, enjoying his pancakes and coffee and giving her time. He'd learned that silence was a greater prompter than any words he could say.

Finally, she said, "I'm adopting the girls and right now I'm their foster mother. But soon I'll be their real mother."

"And they really are sisters?"

Missy giggled again, but it was Steffi who answered. "Yes, we're all sisters, but we didn't get to live together until yesterday."

"You didn't?" He turned to Jennifer. "You mean, the system split them up, or did they move into different homes because they, uh, became available at different times?"

"No, their parents…had an accident. Unfortunately no one foster home could take all three, so they split them up."

"That's barbaric!"

For the first time since he'd met the lovely Jennifer, she smiled warmly at him. "I thought so, too."

"So how did you find them?"

She explained about the photographs for the Heart Gallery.

"And you decided to adopt them at once?"

"Sort of. I'll explain later," Jennifer said in a low voice that made him think of silk sheets and dark nights.

"Uh, okay. These sure are good pancakes."

"I love 'em," Missy said in agreement.

Since she had syrup smeared over half her face, Nick believed her.

"Thank you, Missy," Jennifer said with a smile. "Have you finished?"

Missy nodded.

"How about you, Steffi, Annie?"

"Yes, ma'am," Steffi said. Like Missy, Annie just nodded.

"Okay. I want you to go to the bathroom and wash your face and hands. No sticky parts, okay?"

They nodded, their eyes big.

"Then go to your bedroom. I laid out the clothes for you to put on. If you need help, call me," she added with a warm smile.

Nick thought any kid would want to receive that smile. It certainly worked on the three little girls. They ran out of the room to do as she'd told them.

Again, Nick remained silent. He wasn't sure she would still tell him about the girls.

She looked up. "Do you need more coffee?"

"Yeah, but let me serve you for a change." He picked up her almost empty cup, as well as his own, and refilled them. Then he sat back down.

"When I got ready to photograph the girls, I had

some outfits for them to put on, just for fun. Annie was reluctant. When I reached out for her, I discovered she was covered in bruises. I was so upset, I scared her. She wouldn't tell me how she got them. Finally Steffi told me the mean man at her house pinched her if she didn't do as he said at once."

She swallowed convulsively. "You've seen Annie. Do you think she's a discipline problem?"

"No! How could— Hadn't anyone seen the bruises?"

"Apparently not. I demanded the welfare worker in charge of Annie come at once. She made it six hours later. She, too, was upset by what she saw, but she said she had nowhere else to put Annie. And the charges would have to be investigated."

"So they took her back to the same place?"

"No. She came home with me." She explained about her uncle and all he'd done.

"Do you think you'll be approved to adopt them?" he asked. When she glared at him, he added, "No offense, but I thought a single parent wouldn't be— I mean, usually they look for a couple."

"I'll be approved. My uncle told me they don't turn down qualified applicants."

"I believe the girls will be fortunate if they get you for a mother, Jennifer. I didn't mean any insult."

"I'm a little touchy. My mother— Never mind."

He sat there silently, waiting, hoping she would finish that sentence.

Finally, she said, with a bitter laugh, "My mother thinks I'm ruining my life by adopting the girls."

"She isn't happy to have three granddaughters?"

Again that bitter laugh. "My mother? She isn't interested in being a grandmother in the first place and certainly not a grandmother to children that didn't have her *exclusive* blood."

"Ah, one of the blue bloods, is she?"

"Yes, of course! She was born and bred in Highland Park," Jennifer said, naming an exclusive neighborhood in Dallas, full of prestigious homes and wealthy owners.

"I bet you were a debutante," Nick guessed with a grin.

"Yes. I had no choice. But after I graduated college, I refused to play that role any longer."

"Good for you. Did your mom withhold money to persuade you to change?"

"She tried. I got a job and paid my own way."

"Well, you've certainly done well. These are nice digs."

"Yes, but I wouldn't be here without my grandmother's help."

"Good for her. And you're a photographer?"

"Yes. Not well known yet, but, hopefully, I will be." She took a sip of coffee before she asked, "What do you do?"

He paused, debating his answer. Which one of his careers did he choose? Remembering his agent's stern warning, he chose the less interesting one. "I'm a teacher."

"So you're only here for the summer?"

"Maybe. I'd been thinking about moving to Dallas for a while. I'm going to see what's available."

"You realize if you try to renew the lease next year, the rent will go up, don't you?"

"Yeah."

"I thought I should tell you since I know teachers don't make a lot of money."

"Like unknown photographers?"

She stiffened. "I told you I had help from my grandmother."

"Sorry, that was out of line, anyway. If you'll make me a map, I'll get out of your hair."

"Of course. I'll get pen and paper," she said, still stiff, showing she hadn't forgiven him. Rising, she left the room.

Nick cleaned off the table and loaded the dishwasher.

"What are you doing?" Jennifer asked as she returned.

"Hoping to get you to forgive me," he told her, offering his best smile.

"There's nothing to forgive," she assured him, not meeting his gaze.

"Yes, there is. You've taken me in and fed me twice, and I've repaid you by being rude."

"Please," she said, pushing her chin-length hair behind her ear, "it doesn't matter."

"Jennifer," Missy called out and they both heard the patter of her little feet. Before they could turn around to look, she was in the kitchen with them. "Don't I look beautiful?" Missy demanded, glowing.

Jennifer laughed, a sound full of joy. "You absolutely do, but you should wait for me to tell you, instead of asking."

"But what if you forget?" Missy asked, puzzled by that social rule.

"Well, then I think you could ask." Jennifer reached out to hug the little girl. "Where are your sisters?"

"They're still getting dressed. They had lots of buttons," Missy assured her.

"Okay, maybe I should go help them. And we have to brush your hair."

"Oh." Missy didn't look very happy about that chore. "Sometimes it hurts."

"Bring me the hairbrush and I'll be gentle," Nick promised, smiling at Missy.

"No, I'll take care of it, as soon as I help the others finish dressing," Jennifer assured him, and jumped up from the table to go to the little girls' bedroom.

Nick sat there for a minute, knowing he hadn't gotten his map, but he'd gotten so much more. Just as he started to stand and leave, Missy returned with the hairbrush.

"Don't pull!" she ordered sternly, at least as sternly as a three-year-old could be.

"I won't. Let's move in here," he said, leading the child to the living room. He sat down and pulled Missy onto his lap. "Okay, now, I'm going to be gentle, but if it hurts, tell me."

"Okay!" Missy agreed. She was holding herself stiffly, reminding him of her new mommy. But as he worked on her hair, as he once had his little sisters' hair, she gradually relaxed.

"There, you're all done. Do you have a bow or a barrette to put in your hair?"

"Yes, I have a bow. I'll go get it." She hurried out of the room.

Nick hoped she returned before Jennifer did. When she came running down the hall, he thought he'd be able to finish his job before Jennifer appeared. But she called for Missy just before she reached Nick.

"Missy? Where are you? I need to brush your hair, too."

"Nick did it, Jennifer!" Missy called out and kept running to Nick. She handed him her bow. "Isn't it beautiful?"

"Definitely beautiful." He gently pulled the long hair back and put the bow in place. "Perfect," he said, and bent forward to kiss her on the cheek.

To his surprise, the little girl wrapped her arms around his neck and said, "I love you."

"Missy!" Jennifer said sharply over Nick's shoulder.

The child, with no fear, jumped down and ran to Jennifer. "Don't I look beautiful?" she demanded with a big smile, using what appeared to be her favorite word.

"Yes, sweetheart, you do. I hope you thanked Nick for his hard work."

"I did. Can he come with us?"

"No, we're going to be shopping for clothes, and men don't like to do that. Besides, he needs to go to the grocery store."

"I could do my grocery shopping later," he offered, watching her.

"No. It would be absurd to drag you along on our shopping trip. You'd hate every minute of it."

"Actually, as the oldest child, I had three little sisters, and my mother put me in charge of them often. I would enjoy the shopping trip and you might need help with three of them."

"Please, Mommy?" Missy said, surprising both him and Jennifer.

"That's the first time you've called me Mommy," Jennifer said, looking teary-eyed.

"Is that okay?" Missy asked.

"Of course it is, sweetie," she said, scooping the child up into her arms.

"If you let him come with us, I would hold Nick's hand so he wouldn't get lost," Missy said, her arms around Jennifer's neck. "And he can tell me I look beautiful!"

The other two little girls came down the hall, all neat and tidy, and Nick took the opportunity to praise their appearances also.

"I don't— This is ridiculous!" Jennifer said under her breath.

Nick, however, had an angle he didn't think she

would refuse. "Have you ever thought that it might be good therapy for…someone, to know a man who isn't bad?"

"How do I know you aren't bad?" Jennifer demanded.

"I'm just a teacher who helped raise his three sisters. I'm used to girls. Besides, I'm Grace's nephew."

"Don't you have something better to do with your time?"

"Actually, I don't. This way I'll get to see lots of Dallas and find out where things are."

"Please!" Missy added to his cause.

"Oh, all right, but don't blame me if you get bored!" Jennifer said. She picked up her purse from a nearby table. "Are we ready, girls?"

"Yes," Steffi said, taking Annie's hand. Missy struggled out of Jennifer's hold to come collect Nick. "I'll take care of you, Nick."

"Thank you, Missy," he said, trying to sound like he needed a three-year-old's watchful eye.

Jennifer rolled her eyes and headed for the door.

Two hours later, Nick was impressed with Jennifer's endurance. She still seemed to be enjoying herself. Missy, however, was worn out. She sat curled in his lap while the other girls continued to try on clothes in a nearby dressing room.

"I'm hungry," she complained.

"Me, too. How about I take us all to lunch?"

"Yeah! Can we go to McDonald's?"

"I'm not sure Jennifer would like McDonald's. We'll see."

Just then Jennifer and the other two girls came out of the dressing room.

"Mommy, Nick said he would take us to McDonald's!" Missy said, scooting out of Nick's lap to reach for Jennifer.

"I'll buy you lunch when it gets—" She stopped to look at her watch. "Oh, I had no idea it was almost two o'clock. We'd better take a lunch break, girls."

"Do you have more shopping to do?" Nick asked.

"Yes, but—"

"Then why don't we go to the food court? I'm sure they'll have things the girls will like, and maybe something we can tolerate, too."

"Yes, that's a good idea. Come on, girls. We'll go have lunch. Then we'll shop some more."

When they reached the food court, Nick noticed the McDonald's nearby. "Do you mind if the girls have McDonald's?"

"No, that'll be fine. If you'll stay here with the girls, I'll go get their food."

"You stay with them and I'll go get the food. This meal's on me. It's definitely my turn."

In no time he was back with three Happy Meals and drinks. Then he looked at Jennifer. "Now, what would you like?"

"I'd like a grilled chicken salad and a diet Coke."

"Sounds good. I'll be right back."

He returned with two salads and two drinks.

"I didn't mean you had to get a salad," Jennifer protested as she saw he'd gotten himself the same thing.

"I like salads, too. Though I don't eat a steady diet of them," he assured her with a smile.

"How old are your sisters?" she suddenly asked.

He grinned. "Seven years younger than me."

"All three of them?" she asked in surprise.

"Yeah. My mom had trouble getting pregnant after I was born, so she took fertility drugs and ended up with triplets."

"Oh, my. I guess you do have experience," she said in amazement.

"Yeah. It wasn't until I went away to college that I got to do much of anything by myself."

"What's triplets?" Missy asked.

"It's when your mommy has three babies at the same time," Jennifer said.

Missy nodded, but Steffi looked puzzled. "You mean like us only all the same age?"

"That's right. It makes everything much more difficult. With you being older, you can help your sisters. But Nick had to help all three of his sisters." Jennifer grinned at him. "If you'd told me that earlier, I would've been easier about your helping with the girls."

"I didn't want to brag," Nick said, trying to look modest.

"Yeah, right!" Jennifer said with a laugh.

"How's your hamburger, Annie?" Nick asked. The

little girl had yet to speak to him. He wasn't sure she would speak to him now.

"Good," she replied very softly.

"I'm glad. And yours, Steffi?"

"I like it. And I got a car as my toy."

"Lucky you," Nick said. "And, Missy? What did you get?"

"I got a cat, I think." She held up a plastic figure.

"That's Sylvester the cat. I think they're bringing out a new movie about Sylvester the cat," he said.

"Can we go?" Missy immediately asked.

Her suggestion put a pleasant thought in Nick's head. He and Jennifer in a darkened movie theater—with the girls, of course. Still, he looked straight at Jennifer when he said, "I promise we will."

Chapter Three

"I don't think you have the right to promise that, Nick," Jennifer said, her voice starchy.

"I didn't think a movie would hurt."

Jennifer, however, was more focused on the girls. "Have any of you ever been to the movies?"

Steffi shook her head. Annie just stared at Jennifer, wide-eyed. But Missy nodded.

"When did you go to the movies, Missy?" Jennifer asked suspiciously.

"Once, my old mommy took four of us to the movies and we had popcorn and candy and a Coke!"

"What did you see?" Jennifer asked, watching Missy closely.

"A movie. And we had to be real quiet!"

"Do you remember what happened in the movie?" Nick asked, hoping to help Jennifer.

Missy hung her head.

"Missy?"

She finally looked at Nick and confessed, "I threw up and my old mommy was mad because she didn't get to see all the movie."

"Missy, if it made you sick, why do you want to go again?" Jennifer asked.

"'Cause it was fun. It's real dark and—"

"Never mind. We'll discuss going to the movies when that movie comes out and I can decide if it's appropriate for you."

"What's appropriate?" Missy asked.

Nick answered that question. "If it's a show that's good for you to see. Some of the movies are made for adults and you wouldn't enjoy them."

"Will you let me sit next to you, Nick, if we go to the movies?"

"Sure. We can even hold hands," he told the little girl with a smile.

"We can't expect Nick to come with us, Missy," Jennifer said sternly. "So far, we've managed to take all his time since he arrived. I'm sure he has lots to do. He probably can't come to the movies with us."

Missy turned to Nick, her brown eyes wide, "Please, Nick?"

"I'll try, Missy. But you know how it is. My schedule might get crowded." He stared at Jennifer as he lied to Missy. He thought that was what she wanted.

"Okay. Has everyone finished eating?" Jennifer asked in a cheery voice. When the girls all nodded, she suggested a trip to the bathroom. "Nick, can you guard our bags?"

"I can, but if you'll give me your keys, I could carry them all to the car and put them in the trunk. Then we can load up again when you buy other things."

"Would you mind?" Jennifer asked. "That would be wonderful. We'll be in the children's department again."

"I'll see you there."

He stood there watching as Jennifer led her three little girls to the bathroom. It reminded him so much of his childhood. When the triplets were four and he was eleven, their father had died, and he'd been responsible for the girls in the summer while his mother worked.

It had been hard on all of them, but they'd survived and forged a bond that kept them close. Two of them were married now and the third was living in New York City. He kept up with them, though; after all, it was what his mother asked of him before she succumbed to cancer a couple of years ago.

He shook off thoughts of his family and gathered up the shopping bags. He hoped Jennifer could afford all she was buying. Children were expensive in more ways than clothes.

When he got back to the children's department in the store in which they'd been shopping, he didn't see any of them. But as he drew closer to the dressing room, he heard their voices.

"I want to go outside with Nick," Missy complained.

"Nick is putting our bags in the car. I need you to try on this outfit, Missy. I think it will look very nice on you."

"But—"

"Missy, try on these clothes. Then we'll go see if Nick is back and you can sit with him. Or maybe he can help you find some Sunday shoes and some sandals."

"I get *two* new pairs of shoes?" Missy asked in astonishment. "But I already have these."

He could picture Missy sticking out her feet to show Jennifer her tennis shoes.

"Just try on the clothes. Here, let me help you."

He didn't hear much until Missy spoke up again after a few minutes. "*Now* can I go see if Nick is back?"

"Yes, I'll take you out there. Steffi, you and Annie stay here. I'll be right back."

"I'm here, Jennifer," Nick called. "Just send Missy out. I'll take care of her."

Instead, Jennifer came out with Missy. "Would you mind taking her just across the aisle to find Sunday shoes and sandals?"

"Sure. About what would you like to spend?"

She looked at him blankly. Then she shook her head. "I don't know what little girls' shoes cost. Probably something under fifty. I'll come pay for them in a minute."

Nick shook his head as Jennifer went back into the dressing room. He guessed she didn't have to worry about money. Fifty dollars for kids' shoes? He could do better than that.

In fifteen minutes, he had chosen black patent leather shoes and white sandals for Missy. She was so excited, he had trouble keeping her from charging across the aisle to show Jennifer before he paid for them.

When they got back to the dressing room, he sent Missy in to find Jennifer.

Jennifer came out at once. "Did you tell them I'd be there in a minute to pay for them? I didn't think—"

"I paid for them, but I kept the receipt so you can pay me back. It was just easier that way."

"Oh. I shouldn't— I didn't think— Thank you. I'll write you a check when we get a moment."

"Good. Now, are you ready for me to take one of the others shoe shopping?"

Jennifer frowned. "Annie is ready, but…"

"I'll be very gentle with her and bring her back at once if she gets uneasy, I promise."

"I'll go ask her."

In a minute, Jennifer came back out, holding Annie's hand. "See, Annie? The shoes are just over there. Nick will take you to try some on. Then you can come right back here if I haven't gotten over there yet."

"Okay," Annie whispered.

Nick thought it was a big step for Annie to trust him. He smiled warmly and offered his hand. It would be the first time he had touched her. Her big brown eyes held a lot of fear and hurt, but she slowly put her hand in his.

"Same shoes for her?" Nick asked softly.

Jennifer nodded. "I liked your choices for Missy, by the way. I don't think she intends to take the sandals off even when she goes to bed tonight."

Nick grinned. "She did seem to like them. We'll try to find shoes that will make Annie smile, too. Right, Annie?"

She just stared at him.

He led her over to the shoe section and they looked at what was available in her size. Nick patiently waited for her to make her selection, but she kept watching him, as if afraid she'd anger him if she made the wrong choice.

"Annie, all these shoes are what Jennifer wants you to wear, so you can choose whichever you want to try on. There aren't any bad choices. Just pick the ones you like most."

More silence.

He waited patiently.

Finally Annie pointed to a pair of the dress shoes.

"Good. Are there any others that you want to try on?"

She shook her head. Her hand was trembling in Nick's. He knew this was a big step for Annie. He settled her in a chair and got the saleswoman to bring her size. He also asked for three pairs of sandals to be brought out, all in styles different from Missy's. He'd learned with the triplets to get everyone something different, something that suited their unique personalities.

Annie was quite different from Missy. She showed her enthusiasm with a quiet smile, by touching the shoes in a way akin to a caress. In no time she approved the shoes and picked out a pair of sandals.

"I like these," she whispered, looking down at her newly shod feet.

"Okay, good choice, Annie," he told the little girl, and paid for her shoes. Then he took her back to the dressing room and let her go show Jennifer.

Jennifer came out without Annie. "You did a great job. She's overcome with excitement."

"She has quiet excitement, doesn't she?"

"Yes. I worry that she'll explode if she doesn't learn to express her feelings more like Missy." Then Jennifer grinned. "But I'll admit I might enjoy her excitement better than Missy's some of the time."

"I know. One of the triplets, Elizabeth, was very quiet, too. But she blossomed later."

"You really do have triplet sisters?"

"Yes. Did you doubt me?"

"It just seemed such a perfect story to make me accept you. I began to doubt it as I thought about everything."

He smiled. "Well, it really is true. Is Steffi ready for shoes?"

"Yes, we all are. I'll go get everyone."

After Steffi made her choices and Jennifer bought the shoes, they headed for the car, loaded down with packages again.

"It's a good thing I'm a great packhorse, isn't it?" Nick teased Jennifer as they reached the car. "And a good thing that you have a minivan. Otherwise, all these packages wouldn't fit."

"They'll all fit. If they don't, the girls can put them under their feet."

"I was teasing. But you did buy a lot."

"But the girls had next to nothing. Their clothes were worn hand-me-downs. Missy was so excited last night that she didn't have to share a nightgown."

"They put two kids in one nightgown?" Nick asked in astonishment.

"No. Quit teasing me. They had a community pile of nightgowns. She didn't get the same nightgown every night."

"And now she has a choice of nightgowns, all belonging to her?"

"Yes, and her sisters do, too. They all have enough clothes for the rest of the summer. In the fall they'll be fitted in school uniforms. At least, Steffi and Annie will. Missy will go to a preschool. They don't wear uniforms there."

"What school are they going to?"

"Hockaday. It's where I went to school."

"Okay, I don't have to ask if you're counting your pennies if that's where you're sending the girls," Nick said with a laugh.

"I don't think I ever said I was," she replied stiffly.

"No, but I did wonder as the number of packages grew."

Straightening her back and lifting her chin, Jennifer turned on her heels, mumbling something about checking the girls' seat belts.

What was it about her financial status that angered Jennifer? This was the second time she'd balked when he brought up money. He made a mental note to steer clear of any further comments.

He closed the back of the minivan and hustled around to the passenger seat. He figured he'd better get in before she drove off without him.

On the ride home there was no conversation, until Jennifer pointed out a grocery store.

"There's the one where I shop," she said. "It's only a short distance from the fourplex."

"Yeah, thanks. I'll go later today."

When they reached the fourplex, Nick began gathering packages to carry in to the apartment. Jennifer also came around to the back of the minivan with the girls and gave them each a package to carry in. She gave Steffi the key to unlock the doors.

"Sorry, I should've thought of that," Nick said softly after the girls headed toward the apartment. "It was smart on your part to encourage them to help."

Jennifer raised her eyebrows and put a palm to her chest. "You mean I did something right? With all your experience, Mr. Barry, I guess you would know, wouldn't you?"

"Are you making fun of me, Jennifer?"

"Well, you do seem to think you know better than me."

She was baiting him, but he refused to bite. Instead he complimented her. "Just goes to show that your instincts are good even if you've never had kids before."

Before she could reply, another car pulled into the small parking lot.

"Uh-oh," Jennifer muttered.

Nick looked at the other car. "Is there a problem?"

"Not for you. It's just my mother."

He looked at the woman getting out of the car. She had Jennifer's blond hair, but hers looked artificial. She was dressed in a chic suit and heels, and she wore a lot of gold jewelry. She also wore a frown.

"Jennifer," she called sharply.

"Yes, Mother?"

"Have you lost your mind?" her mother demanded, ignoring Nick, as she approached them.

"I don't think so."

"My brother just complimented me on my daughter's social conscience! When I assured him I didn't know what he was talking about, he informed me that you have applied to adopt three little girls! I won't have it! You must stop this at once!"

"I won't do that, Mother."

"But I won't have it! You'll ruin your life!"

"I'm going to adopt the girls. I believe I'm doing the right thing. And I won't let you tell me what to do!" Jennifer finished with passion in her voice.

"It's your grandmother's fault, isn't it? She made this possible. Otherwise, I'd just cut off your allowance and you'd do what I said!"

"You tried that once, Mother, before Grandmother left me anything, and it didn't work then. It won't work now. I make my decisions, not you!"

"But, darling, you haven't thought this through.

What man will even look at you with three kids tugging on your coattails?"

"I would," Nick said softly, hoping he wasn't going to upset Jennifer.

Jennifer's mother whirled around and stared at him as if seeing him for the first time. "Who are you?"

"He's Grace's nephew and he's leasing the apartment across from me," Jennifer said quietly. "He's a teacher."

"Oh, then he doesn't count. That's not what I have planned for you. Jonathan Davis has shown some interest. But if I tell him about the girls, he'll change his mind."

"Good. I have no interest in Jonathan Davis."

"But, Jennifer, his father is the president of the CMX Corporation. He's worth millions, and his father is worth even more! He's perfect."

"Then I suggest you marry him, Mother, because I have no interest in him!"

"Jennifer, have you lost your mind?" her mother demanded, her hands on her hips, glaring at her daughter.

With her lips pressed tightly together, Jennifer gathered up the last of the packages and closed the back of the minivan. "I have nothing more to say to you, Mother. I can't invite you in because the children would be upset. I'll call you sometime soon."

"You mean I'm not invited into your home?" her mother screamed, outraged.

"That's exactly what I mean! Come on, Nick." Jennifer headed for the front door.

Nick did as she ordered, not bothering to argue with her. He certainly didn't want to have any conversation with the woman who had blown him off. He might no longer be a teacher, but that didn't mean he thought teachers should be so easily dismissed.

When they got into Jennifer's apartment, she collapsed on the sofa, her energy apparently spent in the argument.

The girls came running in, eager to open the packages.

Nick said, "Girls, can you help me take the packages to your bedroom? Your mom is a little tired and needs to rest a few minutes."

Missy and Steffi agreed at once and began gathering packages to take to their bedroom. Annie first went to Jennifer and touched her on her hand, looking at her with big eyes.

"I'm fine, sweetheart," Jennifer said, hugging the little girl. "I just need a few minutes, okay?"

Annie nodded and picked up the leftover packages and silently followed her sisters.

On the way to the girls' room, Nick gave Jennifer a warm, bolstering smile over his shoulder. That was when he noticed the tears glistening in her eyes.

BY EARLY EVENING, JENNIFER had pulled herself together and prepared dinner for her family. When she called the girls in to set the table, Missy asked, "Where's Nick?"

"I'm sure he's at home. He's not part of our family, Missy. You know that."

"But Nick is our daddy! He should be here for supper!" the child said firmly.

"I've told you before, Missy, he's not your daddy. He's our neighbor, that's all." And, she reminded herself, that was all he'd ever be. "Now, help your sisters set the table."

When the phone rang, Jennifer grabbed the kitchen extension, which had a long cord so she could finish fixing dinner while she talked.

"Jennifer?" said a wavery voice she recognized at once.

"Grace, how are you?"

"I'm fine, but I need to pay my rent."

"Uh, Grace, aren't you at the assisted-living facility?"

"Yes, but it's not as nice as my apartment."

"But do you think you'll be able to return to your apartment?" Jennifer asked, confused.

"Oh, yes."

"Have you told your nephew that?" Jennifer asked. Grace Windomere had been a good friend of her grandmother's, which was how she'd gotten the apartment.

"Why would I?"

"If you're subletting the apartment to your nephew, you'll need to tell him."

"What nephew?"

Jennifer froze. Then she said, "Your nephew, Nick Barry. He said you sublet your apartment to him."

"I don't think I have a nephew."

"Grace, are you sure?"

"Well, I should know."

"Yes, you should," Jennifer said, her mind racing. She found it hard to believe that Nick was a brazen liar. But it appeared he was.

Suddenly her breath caught and a wave of cold chilled her body. She'd left her children with the man. Whoever he was. She'd trusted him!

Putting the food on the table, she helped each child serve herself.

"Now, girls, I need to go say something to Nick. You stay here and eat your dinner. I'll be right back. Okay? Steffi is in charge. You do what she says."

With a backward glance, Jennifer hurried out of her apartment and banged on the door across the hall.

When Nick opened the door, she glared at him.

"Grace Windomere doesn't have a nephew!"

Chapter Four

Nick stared at Jennifer. He'd expected a friendly greeting. Not an accusation. Then he pulled himself together and asked gently, "Do you know why Grace is in assisted living?"

"What does that matter?"

He smiled. "She's in the early stages of Alzheimer's disease. She's losing her memory."

"So you thought you could take advantage of her?"

Nick sighed. "Do you want me to show you our family photo albums?"

"I can't take the time. I left the girls eating. But if you have any proof, you can show it to me in the morning or you'll be out of the apartment by noon!" Jennifer turned around and stalked across the hall, slamming her door behind her.

Nick felt like he'd been struck by a whirlwind. A very attractive whirlwind, but an angry one nonetheless. And he had no intention of waiting until morning to prove her wrong.

Because he was the oldest, when his mother died, he'd taken the albums she'd filled with family photos, some of which included his aunt Grace. He hadn't completely unpacked yet, but he searched through the boxes until he found the album that held the older pictures. Then he headed for the apartment across the hall.

After he'd knocked and waited for several minutes, the door opened to Jennifer, still frowning. "What do you want?"

"I want to show you proof that Grace is my aunt."

"How can you do that?"

"With the photos I inherited from my mother. If you'll let me in, that is. Or we could go to my apartment."

"I can't. We're finishing dinner. I have to—"

"Fine. I'll come in," he said, slipping past her, afraid she intended to shut him out.

"But—"

"Hi, girls. How's dinner?" Nick asked as he entered the kitchen.

"It's good," Missy said at once. "But we don't have any left for you, 'cept maybe some green beans," the child said, peering into the serving dishes still on the table.

"I'm not here to eat, Missy, but thank you for thinking of me. I'm here to show some pictures to your mommy."

"I don't remember asking you to come in," Jennifer said from behind him, resentment in her voice.

"I want to get this settled tonight so I don't have it hanging over my head."

"Fine! I'll pour you a cup of coffee. Then I intend to finish my meal. You can just wait!"

With a cup of coffee included, he had no problem sitting at the table. "Thanks," he said, and pulled out the chair next to Missy. "Hello, Steffi, Annie. Did you enjoy your dinner, too?" he asked, careful to add a gentle smile for Annie's sake.

"It was good," Steffi said. Annie just nodded.

Jennifer plunked down a mug of coffee in front of him and took her seat at the table. Ignoring him, she resumed eating her dinner.

Nick thought of the early preparations of his own dinner he'd left behind. He'd done some grocery shopping and had bought a frozen pizza. He'd just taken it out of the freezer when Jennifer knocked on his door. He'd left it on the kitchen counter.

Oh, well, it would be thawed out by the time he got back.

After several minutes of awkward silence, Jennifer said, "I didn't ask if you'd eaten dinner."

"I was fixing it when you…knocked on my door."

She avoided his gaze. "Yes, well, I thought— I trusted you with my children. I'm not used to— I didn't want to think that I'd trusted a liar."

"I don't blame you."

His simple response brought her gaze to his face.

"I—I should've given you a chance to defend yourself."

"It's okay, Jennifer. I understand."

"Quit being so nice! It makes my behavior look bad!" she exclaimed.

He grinned. "That wasn't my intention."

She seethed as she took another bite. "Oh, for heaven's sake, open the album so I can see your proof and then you can go."

"I'm in no hurry. Finish your dinner," he suggested, smiling at her. He already knew she hated the thought of being wrong.

She stood and carried her plate and glass to the sink and disposed of what was left of her dinner. "I'm finished!"

"You're trying to make me feel bad because I interrupted your dinner, but it won't work. You're the one who interrupted me."

"So show me the damned picture and—" She looked up hurriedly at three pairs of innocent eyes. "I mean, if you'll please show me the picture, we can both be satisfied."

Missy stared at her. "My other mommy used to say that word all the time."

"Oh, she talked about pictures a lot?" Jennifer hurriedly said, trying to cover up.

Nick grinned. He was enjoying watching her squirm.

"No, that dammed word. What does it mean?"

Nick could tell by Steffi's face that she knew the meaning. Annie just stared at her dinner plate.

"It's not a nice word, Missy, and none of you should use it. I lost my temper and it slipped out."

"You were mad at Daddy?"

Jennifer drew a deep breath, growing more visibly exasperated by the second. "Missy, you must not call him Daddy. He—"

But Nick saw Missy's sad face and interrupted. "It's okay if we just pretend, Missy. I don't mind."

"Well, I do!" Jennifer returned vehemently.

Silence fell over the room.

"Girls, if you've finished eating, go wash up and I'll put on the movie I was telling you about earlier."

The room cleared almost instantly.

"That must be some movie," he commented.

"It's about a circus. An old Doris Day movie that I loved as a child."

"I remember that one. It was good."

"Yes. Now, show me the picture."

And leave. They were words she left unspoken, but Nick heard them.

Without wasting any more time he opened the album and showed her several pictures of him and his family, including his aunt Grace.

Jennifer went over them with a shrewd eye. "I'm not sure that's really her. It could just be someone who looks like her."

With a sigh, he said, "We could go visit her in the assisted-living facility. Would that convince you?"

"Yes, but I can't leave the kids."

"You don't have someone who could baby-sit them?"

"No."

"Not even a friend who could watch them just for an hour?"

She closed her eyes and he gave her time to think over her friends.

"Maybe, but not tonight. I could try to get someone to look after them tomorrow for a little while."

"Well, if you'll let me stay in the apartment tonight, then we'll go visit Grace tomorrow."

"I suppose so…"

"Are you going to stay and watch the movie with us?" Missy asked Nick as she returned from washing up.

"I'm sorry, sweetie, but I don't think I can. I haven't been invited."

As he'd known she would, Missy began pleading for his presence.

Jennifer held up her hand to stave off her pleas. "Missy, he hasn't had his dinner yet. We can't—"

"All it is is a frozen pizza," Nick said. "If I could cook it over here, we could go ahead and start the movie. I'd love to see it."

Even Annie, who had wandered into the room, clapped her hands at that suggestion. Jennifer drew Annie into her arms and nodded. "Fine. Go get your pizza."

"I'll be right back." He had a suspicion that Jennifer wouldn't let him in again, once he'd left her apartment. So he intended to hurry and get back before she could change her mind.

He really wanted to see the old movie.

At least that's what he told himself.

NICK KNOCKED ON THE DOOR the next day at the appointed time. To his surprise, his knock was greeted with excited barking.

When the door opened, Jennifer appeared ready to leave.

"Wait a minute. I heard barking. Do you have a dog?"

"Yes, we do," Jennifer said with a smile.

"I haven't seen one before. When did you get it?"

"This morning. Now, can we go?"

Missy pushed the door open wider. "Daddy, look at our dog!"

A puppy almost as big as Missy pushed its way into the doorway.

Cries not to let the dog escape, coming from within the apartment, had Nick bending down to impede the animal's progress. "Whoa, there, big guy. Where are you going?"

The dog began licking his hand and trying to jump on his chest, and he petted it as he stood, moving it back into the apartment. "A yellow lab?" he asked Jennifer.

"Yes, blond like the girls."

"And you." He reached out and tugged playfully on her own blond locks. The second his fingers brushed her skin, though, playful took a backseat to exciting. He pulled his hand away.

"Yes, of course. I wanted them to have a pet."

She spoke matter-of-factly as if she was unfazed by the electricity sparking from his light touch. Didn't she feel it? Was he the only one singed from the contact?

Putting a leash on his thoughts, he asked, "Won't he need more room? Dogs of this breed like to run a lot."

"He can run around the backyard. Diane is going to take the puppy and the girls outside and let them play."

"Who's Diane?"

"Diane, come meet your new neighbor," Jennifer called.

A woman approximately Jennifer's age—late twenties—stepped to the door and Jennifer introduced Diane Black the upstairs neighbor living over Jennifer's apartment.

"Are you one of the flight attendants?" he asked.

"No, they live in the apartment over yours. I work at a bank."

"Well, it's nice to meet you. I hope you enjoy spending time with the girls and their new dog."

"We're already off to a great start. Come on, girls, let's take the puppy outside."

Jennifer and Nick watched as Diane took Annie's hand and led the parade toward the back door.

"I haven't even had a chance to look out back. How big a yard is there?"

"It's good-sized. Are you ready to go?"

"After you," he said, and stood back so she could

close the door and lock it. Then he asked, "What made you decide to get a dog?"

"I thought a dog would help the girls believe this is their permanent home. They still have trouble believing they won't be split up again."

"I think you can understand that."

"Of course I can. But I'm doing everything I can think of to settle their minds."

"Except find them a daddy?"

She glared at him as she moved into the sunshine. "We don't need a daddy!"

"I'm convinced," he said with a shrug. "Missy is the one you need to work on."

"It's difficult when you're encouraging her to call you daddy!"

"Sorry, but she's hard to resist."

With a sigh, Jennifer said, "Don't I know it."

"Let's take my car. I need to learn the way so I can go visit Grace on my own."

Jennifer stopped and looked at him. "You would do that?"

He shook his head. "You *are* hard to convince."

"It's not something most men would do on their own."

"Aunt Grace was good to my mother and helped her in the difficult times after my dad died. I kind of feel I owe her."

The explanation obviously satisfied Jennifer because she had no further comments. She got in the car and directed him to the facility.

When they entered, she approached the front desk. "We're here to visit Grace Windomere. Can you tell us her room?"

"Yes, it's 308, but she'll probably be in the main room with the other residents watching television."

"Thank you."

"Aunt Grace never watched much television," Nick murmured.

"Maybe she enjoys it now," Jennifer replied, moving down the hall after they got out of the elevator. They came upon a large room with a big-screen TV.

"There she is," Nick said, pointing across a sea of white hair. He approached her, sliding between the wheelchairs lined up in front of the television.

"Aunt Grace, how are you doing?" he asked softly, kneeling down beside her chair.

She turned to look at him. Then she squealed like a small child. "Nicky! What are you doing here? Is Mary here with you?"

"No, Aunt Grace, Mom is dead, remember?"

"Oh! Oh, yes, I forgot," she said, her eyes filling with tears.

"It's all right, Aunt Grace."

"But the babies!" she protested.

"You mean the terrible triplets?" Nick asked with a grin.

"Oh, yes, right. They were so adorable. Did they come with you?"

"No, they've kind of spread out. But Jennifer, your

neighbor, came with me. You remember her, don't you?"

Jennifer bent over and hugged Grace's neck. "How are you, Grace?"

"I'm f-fine, I guess. I can't seem to find my way home, though. Are you taking care of my apartment?"

"Your nephew is living in it, remember?"

"My nephew?"

"Me, Aunt Grace," Nick hurriedly said. He could see the suspicion come back into Jennifer's eyes.

"Oh, yes, Jennifer. I told Nick he could live there until the lease ran out. Is that okay?"

"Of course it is, Grace. That will be fine."

"And, Nicky, I want you to take good care of Jennifer. She's all by herself, you know. That was my job, but now I live here."

"I'll take care of her, Aunt Grace, I promise." He couldn't stop himself from grinning at Jennifer, knowing he'd see resentment on her face. But he was wrong. He saw tears in her eyes.

Grace turned back to watch the television and he kissed her goodbye, telling her he would come visit again soon.

Jennifer bent to kiss Grace goodbye, too. Then they went back to his car.

Once they were on their way, he looked at Jennifer. "Why did you tear up when Grace asked me to take care of you?"

"My grandmother asked Grace to take care of me. I miss her."

"How long ago did she die?"

"Two years ago."

"That's about when my mother died."

"But you have sisters."

"Yeah, when I see them. One is still in Lubbock, where I was living, one is in Fort Worth, recently married, and one is in New York City."

"New York City? Why?"

"She always had visions of conquering the world, and to her the Big Apple is the world."

"How's she doing?"

"Pretty well, the last I heard."

"But at least you have family," she said sadly.

"Wait a minute. Didn't I meet your mother yesterday?"

"She doesn't count."

"Why not?"

"Because she married my dad for his money. She had breeding, but he had cash. He basically bought her."

"And your dad?"

They divorced. He remarried and had one son. Then he died."

"So you have a half brother?"

"Technically, but the only time I've seen him was at Dad's funeral. I tried to contact my dad before his death, but he told me that his family had nothing to do with me and my mother."

Nick frowned. "That was rather harsh."

"It was to me, but he didn't seem to think so."

Nick couldn't stop himself from reaching out to take her hand in a comforting gesture. When she didn't pull away, he ran his thumb over the top of her hand like a caress. He had to admit, he liked touching Jennifer. Maybe too much.

Apparently so, because she squirmed and turned to look out her window. He put his hand back on the wheel. He needed it to turn, he told himself.

After that, silence loomed, until Jennifer said in a small voice, "Alzheimer's is a horrible disease. I can't believe I didn't see the signs in Grace."

"It's in the early stages. For now she'll be able to stay in assisted living, but there may come a time—"

"I know." She shook her head. "She always seemed okay to me. Sure there were times she forgot things, but—" she laughed "—don't we all? Heck, I forgot my own daughter in the hallway!"

Nick laughed with her and it helped ease the tension. "They're doing remarkable things with medication today. Who knows, maybe Aunt Grace will be one of the lucky ones. Till then, I'll visit her and call her and, if I need to, remind her who I am."

She turned to look at him; he felt her eyes on him and met her gaze. "You're a good man, Nick. I'm sorry I doubted you."

He held her gaze way too long for safety's sake. But he couldn't help himself. Those big blue eyes invited him in, like sirens on the sea, and in them he saw the depth that was Jennifer. The emotion, the character.

Jennifer Carpenter was a complex, feeling woman—and he wanted to take days, months to get to know her every nuance.

He had to settle for a few minutes, because they arrived at the fourplex.

"Back at the ranch," he joked. Then he sobered. "Thanks for coming. I enjoyed the company. Now, will you inform the owners about the lease or shall I?"

"I'll take care of it."

They got out of his car and Nick happened to look at the other buildings on Yellow Rose Lane. "Hey, are those fourplexes, too?"

"Yes. The same architect designed them."

"Do they have the same owner?"

"Yes." Abruptly she started walking toward the building. "I have to go see about the kids now, Nick. Bye."

She hurried inside as if she were retreating from something threatening. He'd only been asking about the other buildings because they so closely resembled the one they lived in. He guessed the builder had figured out he'd run up on a good thing.

As he entered the fourplex he shared with Jennifer, Diane and a bunch of flight attendants, he heard little-girl screams and a puppy barking. Jennifer was receiving a warm greeting.

His own apartment was silent. And that was what he wanted, wasn't it? He'd need the silence to work. Well, maybe not. He'd done a lot of his work with the television on some sports show he didn't want to miss.

Either way, he had to get busy. According to his agent, the second book was supposed to be harder to write. He'd already gotten his proposal approved, and he didn't want to lose the lucrative contract.

It had taken a huge leap of faith to give up teaching and set out as a first-time writer. But Nick had no one else but himself to support, so he took the plunge. His first work landed him an agent and, shortly thereafter, a sale to a major New York publisher.

When they'd bought his second proposal, he jumped at Grace's offer to sublet her apartment and move to Dallas, where he could save money and do nothing but write in a place where no one knew him or what he did.

He didn't mind leaving the bad memories back in Lubbock, either. After all, getting jilted was hard to forget, especially when it had to do with him being a teacher. His fiancé had finally decided he wasn't ever going to make the kind of money she needed and had left him. Nick had thrown himself into his writing, shutting out everything else. He found that story ideas came easily and he had a stockpile of characters he wanted to write.

He only hoped people wanted to read about them.

He looked around for the box that held his computer. No time like the present to get that set up and get to work.

It was time to get his mind off the blonde and onto his book.

JENNIFER HAD INVITED Diane to lunch upon her return. She already had made some chicken salad and now fixed the sandwiches quickly, asking the girls to go wash up while she did so. They'd left the puppy out in the enclosed backyard, happily chewing on a rubber ball.

"Did everything go all right?" Diane asked as she watched Jennifer work.

"Oh, yes, it was fine. He really is Grace's nephew. She has early Alzheimer's and tends to forget things. She asked him about his triplet sisters as if they were still babies."

"He has triplet sisters? My, that must've been fun," Diane exclaimed, sounding lonely suddenly. It reminded Jennifer that she didn't know a great deal about her neighbor.

"Didn't you have any brothers and sisters?"

"No. I was an only child. If I ever marry, I don't intend to have just one baby."

"I don't blame you. But I'm glad my parents didn't have more children. That would just be more people who'd be unhappy."

"My parents were good, but they both had demanding jobs and they enjoyed each other so much, I was kind of an afterthought. Not exactly the way to bring up happy children."

"No, I wouldn't think so."

Jennifer set a plate of sandwiches on the table and poured chips in a bowl.

"Can I help?"

"Sure. Would you get five glasses and fill them with ice? I made lemonade to go with our sandwiches."

By the time the girls got to the table, everything was ready.

"I'm starving!" Missy announced as she plopped down in her chair.

"Me, too," Steffi agreed.

Annie just smiled at Jennifer.

"Aren't you hungry, too, Annie?" Jennifer asked.

Annie nodded.

After everyone was served, Missy said, "I think there's enough left over for Daddy. Do you want me to go see if he's hungry, too?"

"No, Missy, I do not!" Jennifer exclaimed before she calmed herself. "Nick is not your daddy. And he does not have to take every meal with us. He has his own kitchen."

"But—" Missy began.

"Eat your lunch, Missy!"

Diane waited until she thought the girls were occupied before she asked softly, "What does Nick do for a living?"

"He's a teacher."

"And he can afford that apartment on a teacher's salary? They must be getting more than I thought."

"He's getting it at Grace's rate, which is affordable for anyone. When the lease expires in eleven months, I imagine he'll be moving out."

"Oh, I see. Where does he teach?"

"I don't think he's gotten a job here yet. He moved here from Lubbock, I believe he said."

"That's a long way to move without having a job lined up."

"Yes, it is, but I'm sure he'll find something." She refused to worry about Nick Barry. He was a grown man, not some little boy that needed to hang on to her hand.

"Um, why does Missy think—"

Diane's cautious question caught Jennifer's attention. "She seems to think that there's a daddy in every family. Since we didn't have one, she thought she'd snag the first man she found. It was Nick. She wrapped herself around his leg and screamed that she'd found the daddy."

Diane stared at her before bursting into giggles. "And he still speaks to you?"

"Amazing, isn't it?" Jennifer let a smile play about her lips as she remembered the night she first met Nick. "He not only speaks to me, he seems to be involved in this family all the time. He even watched a movie with us last night after I accused him of not being Grace's nephew."

She didn't need to verbalize all his good qualities to realize Nick was quite a man. She'd come to that conclusion a few hours ago. He was kind and considerate, easygoing and attentive. And he had a great sense of humor. Come to think of it, all the attributes she wanted in a man.

But she didn't want a man. Not now. Her life was the girls and being their mother. There was simply no room left for a man. No matter how amazing he was.

"Maybe he's just lonesome," Diane said softly.

"Maybe *you* should ask him out," Jennifer suggested. She did her best to ignore the protest that rose in her throat.

Chapter Five

Several days passed without any contact between Nick and the little family next door. He listened for them going in and out, but he heard nothing.

The only thing to break the monotony of his days was Diane knocking on his door one evening, offering to show him a restaurant or two in the area, if he liked to eat out in the evenings.

Diane seemed very nice and very smart and he didn't want to hurt her feelings, so they went out that night to a nice barbecue place that he enjoyed. He tried to make conversation with her, but mostly he asked questions about Jennifer. Unfortunately Diane wasn't forthcoming.

They parted company at the bottom of the stairs, but there was nothing romantic there. Not like with Jennifer. He hadn't been able to get her out of his head all evening. For days.

Was he crazy? The woman was telling him no as many ways as she could. But he couldn't keep his thoughts away from her. Every movement she made seemed poetic, a thought he'd never had about any other woman. Her smile was like sunshine on a cold day. And she kept him from doing his work too often.

A loud noise out back stopped him from working one afternoon. He got up and went to the bedroom window that looked out on the spacious backyard. Built on a knoll, the house was flanked by a wide deck that covered the entire back of the fourplex. Beyond that was a yard of perfectly tended grass.

When he looked out the window, he saw a big truck pulled up along the fence. A man was arguing with Jennifer in the backyard alongside a stack of boxes.

What had she bought now?

The kids and the dog were dancing around, making conversation difficult, based on the number of times Jennifer turned around to quiet the noisy foursome.

The door to the backyard was in the lobby under the stairs. He left his apartment and moseyed his way out to the deck. He didn't want Jennifer to think he doubted her ability to deal with whatever was going on.

He leaned on the railing, looking down about four feet at Jennifer. Missy spotted him and called up to him at once.

"Daddy! Did you come to play with us? Have you seen how high Blondie can jump?"

The man talking to Jennifer looked up, too. Then, before Nick could get down the stairs, he tossed some papers in her hands and strode out the gate. A few seconds later, they all heard the big truck backing out to the highway.

Jennifer stamped her foot in frustration.

Nick reached her side. "What's up, Jennifer?"

"Nothing! It's none of your business. I don't mean to be rude, but I can handle it."

"Okay, fine." He turned away from her rebuff to find Missy standing beside him. His initial response would've been to be as abrupt with her as Jennifer had been with him.

Instead, he squatted down beside the little girl. "How are you doing, sweetheart?"

"Fine. Did you come down to play with Blondie? She's a lot of fun."

"I can tell. It was nice of your mom to get her for you."

"I know. And Mommy says we won't have to be split up again, so we don't have to divide Blondie ever!" Missy beamed at him.

"That's good for you and especially good for Blondie," he said with a smile. About that time, Blondie discovered a new human to play with. She jumped on her back legs and planted her paws on Nick's chest, trying to lick his face.

Almost immediately, he felt rather than saw Jennifer sweep past him and climb the stairs.

"What's got your mother so upset?"

Missy frowned. "I don't know. She told us she was going to get us a swing set today, but all she got was those boxes."

"Ah. The man didn't put it together."

"You mean that's our swing set? I don't think we can play with it like that."

"No, I don't, either."

Jennifer reappeared on the deck, calling the girls to come in to dinner.

Nick followed the girls up the stairs.

"Hey, Jennifer, do you need some help getting the swing set put together?"

She stared at him, her mouth falling open. Then she snapped it shut. "I don't. The company is going to call me back in a few minutes to schedule someone to come put it together."

"Oh, good. But let me know if you need any help."

"Thank you, but I'm sure I won't need to." With that, she herded the three little girls inside.

Nick was no fool. He knew a brush-off when he heard one.

Clearly he'd upset Jennifer last time he saw her—but he couldn't think of anything he'd done. With a sigh, he climbed the stairs. Life wasn't as exciting without the four—make that five—blondes next door. Though apparently Blondie was being left in the backyard right now.

He knew the feeling.

He returned to his apartment to work. After all, that was why he was here in Dallas. Not to get attached to the family next door. No, definitely not that.

NICK HEARD THE GIRLS playing outside the next afternoon. He wandered to the window to see what they were up to. To his surprise, he discovered Jennifer trying to put together the swing set on her own. And it wasn't going well.

He took his toolbox out of one of the closets and went outside with it. When he reached Jennifer, she was on the verge of tears, dealing with the various parts.

"Hey, Jen, what's up?" he said mildly.

At his voice, she lost her grip on the two parts she was holding and they all collapsed on the grass. "Wh-what are you doing here?"

"I happened to look out and see you working. I thought maybe I could help."

"No, I—I'm taking care of the situation!"

"With that itty-bitty wrench and screwdriver? Could you use some better tools?"

She looked down at the toolbox he was holding out. "What's in there?"

"Tools, of course."

"Why do you have them?"

He blinked several times. "They were my dad's."

"Oh. Would you mind if I used them?"

"Of course you can. But even better, I'll be glad to help you."

"Have you ever put together a swing set before?"

"Sure. When the triplets were eight, Mom bought them a fancy one for their birthday. I was fifteen. It was my job."

She kept staring at him, and Nick didn't know what she was looking for. He waited patiently.

She abruptly said, "I'll pay you to put this together," and motioned to the pile of boxes on the ground.

He frowned. "That's not necessary. I can—"

"No! I have to pay you."

Nick studied her for several minutes. "Okay, you can pay me."

"Do you want a set fee or an hourly wage?" she asked in a businesslike tone.

"Definitely a set fee."

Her eyebrows soared. "What did you have in mind?"

"Dinner and a movie."

"You mean a date?" she asked in outraged tones.

"Yeah, with you and the girls. I want the dinner homemade, and the movie something the girls will enjoy."

"That's not a good idea," Jennifer said, actually taking a step backward.

"Why?"

"Because it enforces Missy's belief that you are a part of the family!"

"But I don't stay there at night," he pointed out.

Jennifer took two steps back. "I'm not having this conversation!"

Then she turned around and ran up the stairs.

After watching her run away, Nick turned around and found three little girls staring at him.

"Did you hurt Mommy?" Steffi demanded.

"Of course not. At least, if I did, I didn't mean to."

Missy came to his side. "Mommy is unhappy."

He squatted down beside her. "I know, sweetheart, but I was trying to help."

"Okay."

Annie hadn't moved. He smiled at the little girl, but he didn't reach out to her. "How about I put together the swing set while y'all play with Blondie?"

All three girls clapped their hands together.

Nick got started putting the swing set together, warning the girls to keep their distance because he didn't want them to get hurt.

Steffi and Missy raced down the yard, Blondie keeping pace with them. Annie sat on the bottom step of the stairs to the deck, staring at Nick.

He had no idea why she wasn't playing with the others. But he asked no questions. Instead, he got busy putting the swing set together. Compared to the one he'd put together for his sisters, this swing set was simple, but it was appropriate for the three little girls. It had two swings, a two-seated glider and on the end, a wavy slide.

Half an hour later, he heard the sound of footsteps coming down from the deck. He didn't look around. It could only be Jennifer. If she told him to stop, that's what he'd have to do, but he was so close to finishing it, he hoped she'd forgive him and let him finish.

WITH A MOTHER LIKE HERS, Jennifer knew guilt. But none was as heartfelt as the guilt that she felt now. She'd treated Nick badly, had ignored him, been short-tempered with him. Yet here he was, outside on a scorching day putting her children's set together.

She owed him. Big time. A lot more than the glass of icy lemonade she was bringing him.

She should've brought one for herself. Hadn't she heard somewhere that lemonade went well with crow?

Intending to give him the drink, say her piece and leave, she called his name. But when he turned around, the only sound she uttered was a gasp.

Nick had removed his shirt and for the first time she saw his muscles and broad chest. In the midday sun his pecs and six-pack glistened like Cortez's gold. She stood there, her mouth agape, her mind blank. She'd wanted to tell him something, but she couldn't think what. All she knew was that he hadn't gotten those muscles from teaching school!

She closed her mouth and swallowed, snapping herself out of her trance. "Thank you for ignoring my rudeness and helping me out." But her gaze kept drifting to his impressive chest.

He smiled slightly. "No problem."

"Yes, it is a problem. You've been very generous with your time and your patience." She looked at Missy and Steffi playing with the dog. It was a safer sight than his rippled abs.

"Look, Jen, it's no big deal. I like putting things together."

"I'm fixing steak for dinner and I'll go pick up a movie. Do you have any requests?" Regardless of the movie, she didn't intend to watch. She'd find something else she needed to do.

"I wanted to see *The March of the Penguins* a couple of years ago, but somehow I missed it. Would the girls like that one?"

"They'd love it. Is there anything else you want for dinner?"

"Nope. Everything you cook is good, Jen. Whatever you make will be fine."

She began backing away, trying to force her gaze to something, anything else, rather than Nick. "Th-then I'd better go work in the kitchen. Thank you again."

She reached the stairs to go up to the deck and discovered Annie sitting on the bottom step. The child whispered something to Jennifer that had her reluctantly looking back at Nick. She returned to his side.

"I'm sorry to ask— I mean, it may slow down what you're doing, but Annie— She's interested in how things fit together. Would you mind showing her what you're doing?"

"No, I'd be glad to. Annie? Could you come help me a little?"

Annie stared at him warmly, obviously weighing her decision. Then she jumped up and ran to him. For the first time that day, she spoke to him. "Yes?"

"I just need a little help. All these screws get mixed up, see?" He held up the instructions and pointed to a diagram. "I'm looking for this screw. Can you find two just like it?"

Her face lit up and she nodded vigorously.

"Great." He stood there smiling at the little girl's intent search.

Jennifer guessed Annie was like Nick. She enjoyed putting things together. If Nick could help the girl grow more confident, maybe it would be worth risking a little time with him.

But could she resist the temptation?

NICK WATCHED ANNIE'S CONCENTRATION as she searched through the screws to find that one that was missing. One of the triplets was like that. She always wanted to help. Nick found teaching his sisters how to do things easier than he had found repairing broken hearts. With three sisters, he got better at that, but he never got comfortable with it.

Jennifer seemed to need some help, too, but he wasn't sure what to do. He just felt she needed something. And he was a little distracted by the sundress she was wearing. Its color matched her blue eyes.

"I found them," Annie whispered, holding the two screws out for him to see.

"Good job, Annie. Now, do you want to see what I'm going to do with those two screws?"

She nodded her head and squatted on the ground right next to him, her gaze fixed on his hands.

The rest of the afternoon, Nick and Annie worked together. He let her use the screwdriver and the wrench. He never had to repeat his instructions; she remembered everything.

About four o'clock, he declared that they were done. Annie stood beside him, staring at the swing set. Her two sisters ran up, the dog accompanying them.

"Is it ready?" Missy asked.

"Yes, but before you try it out, Annie gets to go first."

Annie looked up at him in shock. Then with a smile, she stepped forward and reached for the first swing. Nick helped her into it.

"Are you ready, Annie?"

She nodded.

He gently pushed her and she closed her eyes, feeling the motion. "Do you like it, Annie?" he asked.

"Oh, yes. Push me higher." Her voice was still low, almost a whisper, but he heard her. He pushed her a little harder.

"*We* get to play, too," Missy demanded.

"Only when Annie says. She worked with me while you two played. That's why she gets to go first."

Annie opened her eyes and said clearly, "I think they should get to play, too."

Missy and Steffi screamed and got on the two-seated glider.

Nick sat down on the steps so he could keep an eye on the girls and enjoy their enthusiasm.

After almost an hour, he heard footsteps above him. He leaned back and looked up the stairs. Jennifer had arrived.

"You finished! And it looks great," she said.

"Yes, Annie and I did a good job."

Annie jumped out of the swing she had occupied from the beginning and ran up the stairs to wrap her arms around Jennifer's legs.

"Mommy, I helped! I really helped!"

Jennifer knelt down and hugged Annie. "That's wonderful, sweetie! You and Nick did a great job."

"Thank you. I learned lots from Nick."

"That was nice of Nick to show you things."

"Yes!" Annie beamed at Nick.

"Girls, come join Annie. It's time to clean up for dinner. Nick is going to be our guest tonight. Then we'll watch a movie."

The girls cheered, flashing smiles at Nick as they raced up the stairs. None of the smiles glowed like Annie's. None touched his heart the way hers did.

His eyes followed the girls all the way up, then lit on Jennifer.

"You really reached her, Nick," she said, her voice quavering. "I knew a special person lived under that quiet, shy exterior, but you brought her out."

Overcome with excitement, she threw her arms around his neck, nearly toppling him. He stumbled back and braced himself, using his hands on her waist to right her.

Lord Almighty, she felt good. He could stay like this all day, burning up under the hot sun, growing even hotter with Jennifer's body against his.

Apparently, she thought differently. As abruptly as she embraced him, she dropped her arms and stepped back. Her face was ashen before she turned and fled up the stairs. "Half an hour, Nick," she threw over her shoulder as she ran.

Half an hour. That'd just give him enough time to shower.

And, boy, did he need a shower.

An ice-cold one.

NICK LAUGHED AT THE ANTICS of the penguins with Jennifer and her girls. But when the movie ended, only he and Jennifer were still awake. He helped her carry the girls to bed. Fortunately, she'd already had them brush their teeth and dress in their pajamas.

Coming out of the girls' room, he feared Jennifer intended to walk him straight to the door. All throughout the movie, he'd got the sense she'd prefer him to be anywhere but in her apartment. Twice, in fact, she'd left the room and he had to go find her and bring her back. To forestall his departure, he asked, "Any chance of a cup of coffee?"

"You want caffeine at this hour?" she asked in surprise.

"No. I hoped maybe you had some decaf."

"Of course," she said, and led the way into the kitchen. "You can go sit in the living room, if you want. I'll bring it in in a minute."

"That's all right. I like your kitchen." He pulled out a chair and sat down.

"Okay," Jennifer agreed, but her voice reflected some doubt.

He watched her move swiftly, putting on a pot of coffee. Then she took cookies out of the cookie jar and put them on a saucer in the middle of the table.

"I think these will go well with coffee."

"I think they'll go well with most anything. You are a great cook, Jen."

"Thank you, but I suspect you know your way around the kitchen, too. You seem to do everything well."

"I don't know the variety of recipes you do. I'll admit I can bake cookies, but I'm not so good with the vegetables." He smiled at her, hoping to tempt her to smile.

She avoided his gaze and got down the coffee mugs.

After she filled them, Jennifer returned to the table and set his in front of him before she sat down across from him.

"You did a great job on the swing set, Nick. In spite of my rude behavior, I really appreciate you spending the afternoon doing that. Especially because of what you did for Annie. I couldn't believe that she'd rather help you than play with the other girls."

"One of my sisters was like that. She was fascinated with putting things together. Still is. She has her own power tools and does all the repairs around the house. Her husband is hopeless at it."

"Really?"

"Yeah. She threatens to teach classes to women who are married to men like Joe."

"It sounds like a good idea."

"Yeah. So any time you need something fixed, just knock on my door."

"Oh, no, I couldn't! I already have a plumber and an electrician that I usually use."

"Well, maybe in an emergency."

"Yes, that—that's very nice of you."

Then they sat there, neither having anything to say.

Finally he asked a question that was none of his business, but he'd wondered. "Have you ever contacted your half brother to see if he's interested in getting together?"

"No. I assumed my father told him my mother and I were not the kind of women he would be interested in."

"How old was he when your father died?"

"I think he was twelve."

"How long ago was that?"

"Seven years."

"And you've never contacted him in all that time?" he asked in surprise.

"No. I thought about it, but…I doubt a nineteen-year-old would care about a half sister." She took a sip of her coffee, then blurted, "I don't want to talk about this anymore."

"I see. Okay, I'd better go so you can get to bed early. That's what you want, isn't it? Not to have me around any longer than you have to?"

She appeared shocked by his words.

Without saying anything else, he stood and walked to the door, calling out good-night over his shoulder.

SHUTTING AND LOCKING THE door, Jennifer rested her forehead against the cool wood. She felt terrible. She'd hardly been the perfect hostess tonight. Hardly been a decent human being, trying to sneak out of her half of the bargain. Had Nick asked too much—dinner and a movie—in return for setting up the swing set?

She lightly rapped her forehead against the door. Maybe it'd knock some sense into her head. What was wrong with her?

A small voice behind her called her name.

"Steffi, what are you doing up? Did I wake you?"

"No, it's not your fault, Jennifer." She sounded so mature, well beyond her years.

"What is it, then? Can't sleep?"

"I—I had a dream. A nightmare, actually." She lowered her head and Jennifer thought she heard a sniffle. Before she could reach out to her, Steffi ran to her and wrapped her arms around her hips.

"What is it, sweetie? You can tell me."

Steffi let the tears come. She whispered, "I dreamt of them again. My parents…in the accident."

Jennifer knelt down and took the child into her arms, cradling her head and wiping her tears. Fresh ones wet her cheek with each sob. "Steffi, it's okay—"

The girl raised her red eyes to her. "No, it's not! You don't understand!" Her voice rose and Jennifer feared she'd become hysterical. What should she do?

She carried Steffi to the sofa and sat down. Wiping her long blond hair from her eyes, she took the girl's cheeks in her palms. When she saw the sadness that racked Steffi, she couldn't stop her own tears from falling. "Why don't you tell me about it, sweetie? What's in your dream?"

Steffi nodded. "It's dark, past our bedtime…but I sneak out of bed and walk down the road. I see Mommy and Daddy's car heading toward home…." Her voice hitched. "Then a big truck crashes into them from out of nowhere. I'm screaming for them and I run to their car….

"That part of the dream is always the same. I run to the car and find them." A sob stole her voice then and robbed her of breath. When she steadied herself, she said, "But for the past month every night I run farther and farther to get to the car. Tonight I never got there."

She looked into Jennifer's eyes and fresh tears bathed her cheeks. "I never saw them. Not tonight."

Jennifer wished the social workers had included grief counseling in their brief session when she'd gone to pick up the girls. She certainly needed it now. But she'd had no idea that Steffi suffered so much, that she was up every night with terrible nightmares. She followed her instincts.

"Steffi, I think it's part of the process of grieving—of losing your parents. You may not reach them in your dream, but you'll always have them in your heart."

Steffi nodded but she clearly wasn't mollified. "But I'm forgetting what they look like. I can't close my eyes and picture them anymore."

Jennifer felt her heart break in two. Overcome by

the child's grief, she could only take her in her arms and cry with her.

After a few minutes, she got an idea. "Do you have any pictures of your parents?" she asked.

Steffi shook her head. "The lady who took us from our house didn't let us take much."

How horrible, Jennifer thought. To lose your parents and your home at such a young age. Plus, she knew how seriously Steffi took the role of older sister. On top of all her emotional pain, Steffi still had to be strong for Annie and Missy.

Someone needed to be strong for her now. Not someone. Her.

"I tell you what," she soothed, forcing a facsimile of a smile. "You leave it to me and I'll see what I can do about getting a picture for you so you won't ever forget them." First thing tomorrow morning she'd put in a call to social services and to her uncle. "Okay?"

When Steffi nodded, Jennifer stood up. "Now, let's get you back to bed."

After she had kissed Steffi good-night, she went back into the kitchen. Absently she took a sip of her leftover coffee and spit it into the sink when she found it ice cold. She plopped into a chair and buried her face in her hands, letting her tears flow freely.

Whatever had led her to believe she could do this? What skills did she have to be a mother to Steffi, Annie and Missy?

She fell to pieces at their pain, didn't have the

answers to make everything all right. Wasn't that what a parent was supposed to do? A good parent, anyway.

Before this, her life was in complete control. She'd been able to handle every crisis that occurred, though admittedly there weren't many of them.

But with the girls, problems seemed to pop up often. She was struggling to keep herself organized and take care of everything.

What if she couldn't do it? What if she failed as a mother? In the past, if she had an off day, it only affected her. Now an off day affected Steffi, Missy and Annie. Jennifer couldn't allow that, not when the girls had already suffered so much.

Normally, she was a glass-half-full person, but now being positive seemed impossible. She was in way over her head. And she was drowning.

Not only with the girls but with Nick.

No matter how she tried, she couldn't deny the attraction she felt for Nick Barry. She was drowning, all right. Going down for the third time, with no life raft in sight. As a new mother she had no business thinking about a man! She would banish the attraction from her thoughts—it simply had no place in her new life. Drawing a deep breath, she relaxed her fists.

No matter what happened, she vowed she would keep her family together. She wasn't going to be like her father or her mother. But that fear had been growing in her. The first day had been easy, but the girls asked questions she couldn't always answer. Especially Missy, asking about Nick.

And now she'd been rude to Nick again.

She decided that was at least one thing she could correct easily enough. Drawing another steadying breath, she got up and headed for Nick's apartment.

It took several minutes for him to answer. But she wasn't giving up. She knew he was in there.

Finally he opened the door. He didn't say anything, though, just stood there, staring at her, waiting for her to make the first move.

"Nick, I'm sorry!"

"For what?"

Okay, so he was going to make her spell it out. That was fine. He deserved an explanation.

"I was rude to you again. I've—I've never— I'm afraid I'm not going to be a good mother."

He stared at her. "Are you crazy? Of course you're going to be a good mother!"

"No, I'm not!" she said, and burst into tears.

Chapter Six

Putting together the swing set was easier. Hell, building the Great Pyramids was probably easier. But just like with his sisters, Nick wouldn't back away from comforting a sobbing female. He gingerly put his arms around Jennifer and patted her back. She just turned into his chest and cried even more.

He tried consoling her with words. "It's okay, Jen. You're just under a lot of pressure."

But she didn't seem to hear him over her sobs.

She resisted when he tried to draw her into his apartment, so he moved them both into her apartment and guided them to the sofa.

Still, she refused to look at him. She buried her face in his shoulder, still crying. For a while, he just held her. "You're a great mother, Jen. I know that and the girls know that." If he wasn't mistaken her sobs began to ease. "Whatever you think is wrong, can surely be corrected. All it takes is love and time. Come on now," he soothed, "tell me. Are you having problems?"

"I don't seem to have answers for everything," she said with a hiccup.

"You don't have to."

At that she sat up and stared at him. "I—don't?"

"Nope. Just because you're a mom, that doesn't mean you're not a human being anymore. No one has all the answers, Jen, no matter how much we wish we did. All you can do is love the girls and let them know you'll always be there for them."

"That's—that's rather a simplistic approach, isn't it?" she said.

"Look, I'm not a parent, but I do know most parents start out with one child at a time. Even if they have three at once, they're little babies for a year. You've taken on three at once, but all three can talk and make demands and ask questions. It's not that you're not going to be a good mother. It's that the kids have a head start on you."

"You really think so, Nick?"

He nodded. "I know so. You've got those maternal instincts in spades." He wiped away her tears. "If you doubt yourself, why don't you call Child Services and see if they offer parenting classes? Or maybe the YWCA has classes. There's got to be one somewhere."

"But then I'd have to hire a baby-sitter and I don't even know any."

"You know me."

"Yes, but— You mean you'd baby-sit for me?"

"Sure. I love being with the kids."

"That's very generous, but it's not fair to you."

"I'm the one offering. It's no big deal."

"O-okay. I'll check on those classes tomorrow. And I'm sorry I cried."

He smiled at her. "It's just nature's way of releasing tension. It's good for you."

"Did your sisters cry a lot?"

"Of course. They were girls. I think girls are lucky that it's okay for them to cry. Guys have to go work up a sweat to get any release."

"Crying is very messy."

He leaned over and grabbed a tissue from a box on the lamp table, shocked when she allowed him to dry her tears. "Messy looks good on you."

Her cheeks flushed and she jumped to her feet. "I won't keep you, Nick. Thanks for helping me again. I'll try not to make a habit of it."

Nick stood. What choice did he have? "I figure I'm storing up credit for when I need help."

"O-of course. Just let me know."

"Good night, Jen. I'll see you soon."

She didn't answer.

JENNIFER FELT GUILTY.

She'd found a great parenting class that would go on for six weeks. Tonight had been her first meeting and she'd loved it. Already she'd learned so much.

But that wasn't the reason she was tiptoeing into her apartment. She hadn't told Nick, or taken him up on his offer to keep the kids. Instead, she'd called an old girl-friend and found out what sitter she used. After inviting the sixtyish woman to lunch to see if she and the kids got along, Jennifer had asked the woman to baby-sit twice a week for the duration of the lessons.

She hadn't taken Nick's generous offer.

She'd rather he didn't know, and that was the reason for tiptoeing. She inserted her key in the lock, opened the door and slipped inside. Breathing a sigh of relief, she turned and greeted Mrs. Peters, who was watching television.

"Mrs. Peters, how did it go tonight?"

"Just fine. The girls are lovely. I'll be happy to baby-sit anytime you want."

Jennifer smiled. "Well, I think twice a week will be fine, but I'll let you know if anything else comes up."

She paid her the money, a generous amount because she wanted the best baby-sitting possible, and said good-night to the woman.

Just as she was going out the door, Mrs. Peters stopped. "Oh, there is one thing. Your neighbor across the hall, Nick—a lovely man, I might add—stopped by. The girls seemed very happy to see him. Missy kept calling him Daddy, which confused me until he explained it was just a game they played. Even Annie seemed happy to see him, and, as you said, she's dreadfully shy."

"I see. What did he say?"

"About what?"

Jennifer wanted to yell at the woman, but that would've been impolite. "What did he say about finding you baby-sitting?"

"Why, nothing, except that he could tell I was doing a good job." The woman beamed at her, then, saying good-night, closed the door behind her.

So sneaking in hadn't mattered! Nick found out, anyway.

"Damn it, now I owe him another apology!" Then she looked around guiltily to be sure no one had heard her remark. It would be just her luck for Missy to pop out from behind a door to catch her.

Maybe she should just not apologize, let the distance between them grow. She didn't *need* him to be a part of her life. He was only a neighbor, not a boyfriend or the father of her children.

What a nightmare that would be!

The only problem was the kids liked him.

And so did she. She hadn't dated in a while because her mother had pushed her so determinedly toward an "eligible bachelor." Which in her mother's lexicon meant a wealthy, socially placed bachelor. But she'd enjoyed his company. And she'd miss him if he went away.

Admitting that made her creep across the hall and rap softly on his door. If he didn't answer, she could talk to him tomorrow but—

He swung open his door. "Yes?"

Jennifer could hear the stiffness in his voice.

She sighed. "I know you came over and met Mrs. Peters."

"Yes. I didn't mean to intrude, but—"

"Nick, I owe you another apology."

"Not at all. I'm just a neighbor."

She could hear his unspoken comment. He would keep to himself. That would be better for him. He could play with the flight attendants upstairs and have a lot more fun. But that wasn't what she wanted anymore.

"Will you join me in a cup of decaf coffee?"

He seemed surprised by her invitation. After a pause, he agreed and came across to her apartment.

Once they each had a mug of coffee in front of them, she said, "I'm sorry I didn't tell you about Mrs. Peters before tonight. I felt guilty about using her instead of you, but I owe you so much already, I just didn't want to impose. And now, if I want to go someplace without the girls, which the teacher of our class said was healthy, not selfish, then I have a sitter available."

"Great." There was no enthusiasm in his voice.

"Nick, don't you understand?"

"Sure I do. You don't need me."

"You're talking as if we'd been married, or had lived next to each other for years! What's it been, four, five days?"

He shrugged his shoulders.

"You should be happy that you're not tied down to me and three kids!"

"Look, I know I've kind of thrown myself into your

situation, but I—I miss my family. My mother's gone and the girls have spread out and made their own lives, as they should, but suddenly, again, I felt like I had a family. I made too much of it. I'll back off and stay out of your lives."

"No! What I'm trying to say is that we enjoy having you in our lives. Annie even talks about you now. You've become a friend very quickly and you've helped me make it through some tough times. But I'd like our friendship to be a two-way street. I'd like to help you as much as you help me."

"Help me with what?"

"I don't know. But our friendship can't continue if it's all going to be so one-sided!"

"But that's just it. It isn't one-sided. I get to feel like I have a family again. That's a great gift, Jen."

"Can't I help you, uh, clean, or cook or—"

"You could take my picture."

She stared at him. "Why?"

"I need it for my job. A nice picture, you know, like the ones you were taking of the girls. I need one, and I don't know where to go."

"I'll be glad to take your picture. When?"

"Tomorrow?"

"Okay. The girls go to their room to rest or nap after lunch. Why don't you join us for lunch?"

"That would be too much."

"Not for friends."

"Okay, but I'll pay you for the picture."

"Not between friends."

"Okay, not the actual taking of the picture, but the processing and the paper. That can't be between friends."

She nodded her consent. "If you want to be photographed with a suit and tie, just bring them with you. My studio is in the third bedroom."

"That would be great, Jen. Thanks."

"I feel better now that we've worked things out. It just made me uneasy for everything to be so one-sided."

"I agree. And you've greatly relieved my mind." He stood. "Guess I'd better go get some beauty sleep, hadn't I?"

With a chuckle, she agreed, standing to follow him to the door. Once the door was opened, he turned suddenly, as if he'd forgotten something.

She looked up at him, wondering what it could be. Suddenly, his lips covered hers in a brief but very pleasant kiss.

"Good night," he said, and closed her door behind him.

"G-Good night," she whispered when she could find her voice. She leaned back against the wall, not sure she could stand without support. His kiss had her totally undone. Her lips still burned from his and she blew out a sigh.

This wasn't quite what she had in mind when she spoke about a two-way relationship.

NICK SUSPECTED THAT Jennifer would be a little miffed by his kiss. But he'd been dying to taste her soft lips since he'd first met her. What was one little kiss, anyway?

He didn't want to answer that question. He should never have touched her. He'd told himself that all of their contacts had been because he was lonesome, but he hadn't sought out other people. Only Jennifer and her little girls. He needed to be concentrating on his own life, not theirs.

That resolve lasted until the next morning when he phoned her to find out what time she wanted him there for lunch. To his surprise, Missy answered the phone.

"Good morning, Missy, it's Nick. Is your mommy home?"

"Hi, Daddy! When are you coming over?"

"That's why I'm calling. I don't know what time I should come."

"You're really coming over?" Missy asked, excitement in her voice.

"Yes, I—"

"Hello?" Jennifer suddenly said. "Who is this?"

"It's Nick. What happened to Missy?"

"I took the phone away from her. She's too young to answer the phone."

"That's true. I just wondered what time you wanted me there for lunch. I don't want to be late."

"Twelve o'clock will be fine."

She didn't sound friendly, but he guessed that was his fault. "Fine, I'll be there at twelve. And I really appreciate you doing this, Jen."

"Okay."

Definitely not friendly. Surely she'd been kissed before. Or... The thought struck him like a lightning bolt. Did she have a boyfriend? He didn't think so. After all, her mother kept trying to fix her up with some rich stiff.

One thing was certain: it was time to talk about her past.

After hanging up the phone, he gathered a suit jacket and tie and a dress shirt on a hanger. And he chose a sweater he particularly liked, for a more casual look. He thought the sweater might be a better look, but he could get Jennifer to take a couple of pictures so he'd have a choice.

He found himself ready long before noon. Then he paced the living room of his apartment, waiting until it was time to go over to Jennifer's. Fortunately, it was a nice-size living room and his aunt had excellent taste. She'd furnished it with a lot of leather, which he loved.

He checked his watch again.

Five minutes. He wanted to see Jennifer again. And he was dying to kiss her again. Therein lay the problem with having kissed her last night. He suddenly had a raging thirst for Jennifer Carpenter...when he should be working on his future.

Okay, time was up. His hunger for Jennifer would ease, just being around her, wouldn't it?

He was pretty sure it couldn't grow stronger. It was at hurricane level already.

Crossing the hall at exactly twelve o'clock, he knocked on the door.

Jennifer swung it open and he had to fight not to greet her with a kiss. It seemed so natural, so right.

"Hi, Nick. Come in."

"I hope I'm not too early."

"No, not at all. Here, let me take your— Oh, you brought two outfits?"

"Yeah, I hope you don't mind. I'm not sure what will look right."

"Of course."

Missy came running into the room. "Hi, Daddy!"

"Hello, sweetheart," he said, swinging her up into his arms. She squealed with laughter.

"Missy, show some decorum!" Jennifer snapped.

Missy didn't understand the word, in Nick's opinion, but she did understand that tone of voice. She stiffened and then wiggled out of Nick's hold.

"I'm sorry, Mommy, but I'm glad to see Daddy and—"

"No! I mean, he's not your daddy. Why don't you call him Nick?"

"But he *said* I could call him daddy."

Afraid of losing a lot of ground, Nick knelt down beside Missy. "Mommy's right, and I was wrong. That's a special word that you need to save until you get a real daddy. If you call me Nick, it will be like we're friends. Okay?"

"Okay," she said solemnly.

He looked up at Jennifer, to see her struggling. He stood. "Is everything all right?"

"Yes, of course."

"Mommy, it smells like something's burning," Steffi called from the kitchen. Jennifer turned and hurried to the kitchen.

Missy slid her little hand into Nick's. "I liked calling you Daddy."

"I know, honey, but it upsets Mommy. And if she decides it's not good for me to visit, then we wouldn't get to see each other."

"Would she do that?" Missy asked in horror.

"I hope not."

"Okay, I'll call you Nick, but I'll be thinking Daddy."

Nick smiled. "Okay, that's a deal."

The two of them entered the kitchen to find Jennifer taking a dish of macaroni and cheese out of the oven. "Smells good, Jennifer."

"I'm afraid it's not fancy."

"Fancy's not necessary. Where did you learn to cook, by the way? After meeting your mother, I can't see her slaving over a stove."

Jennifer's shoulders stiffened. Uh-oh, he'd made another mistake.

"My mother may not be the homemaker type, but she hired very good people to cook and clean. And I learned a lot from our cook."

"You're certainly an accomplished cook," he said, adding a smile to get in her good graces.

"Lunch is ready. Please be seated."

Obviously his smile hadn't worked. He pulled out a

chair and sat down at the place she'd indicated. To his surprise, Annie came over to greet him.

"Hi, Annie. How are you doing?"

"Fine." She beamed at him.

"Tomorrow is Annie's birthday," Steffi announced.

"It is? And you'll be six?"

Annie shook her head no and held up five fingers. Nick frowned. "I thought you said she was five?" he asked Jennifer.

She shrugged. "It was so close to her birthday, we aged her already. But tomorrow is the big day."

"Well, congratulations, Annie. You'll make a great five-year-old," he assured her with a big smile. Annie nodded her head, still beaming at him.

"What are you getting for your birthday?"

Annie frowned and then turned to her mother.

"I think Nick means what do you want as a gift. You get a present on your birthday," Jennifer explained.

"I do?" Annie's eyes lit up with excitement. "I want a dolly!"

Jennifer bent down and kissed Annie's cheek. "Then a dolly it shall be."

Annie stared at Jennifer. "Really?" she asked in a whisper. "I get a dolly?"

"Really, sweetheart," Jennifer promised.

Annie got in her chair and stared into space, a smile on her lips.

"I think she's picturing her dolly. I don't envy you in trying to pick the right one." Even as he spoke, Nick was thinking about what he would get for Annie. He'd be doing some shopping this afternoon, he guessed.

"When do I have a birthday, Mommy?" Missy asked.

"You will be four next September, Missy," Jennifer answered as she finished bringing the food to the table.

"Is that tomorrow, too?" Missy asked.

"No, honey, September is when school starts and the leaves on the trees begin to turn."

"But I want a dolly, too!" Missy protested.

"Well, I think, since Annie has the first birthday, it would be all right if you got a small present, you and Steffi," Jennifer said.

"Would it be fun if we went to Chuck E. Cheese's for your birthday party, Annie?" Nick asked, hoping Jennifer would agree so he could help celebrate Annie's birthday.

"What's Chuck E. Cheese's?" Annie asked.

"It's a pizza place with lots of games for you to play after you eat pizza."

"I like pizza," Annie said, looking at Jennifer hopefully.

After drawing a deep breath, Jennifer said, "I guess we could do that. And I'll bake a special cake for you, Annie."

"I get a cake, too? And a dolly?" Annie asked, her eyes as big as saucers.

Jennifer hugged her again. "Yes, sweetie."

"When's my birthday?" Steffi asked.

"You had a birthday in March," Jennifer said.

"But I didn't have a cake or a dolly," Steffi pointed out.

Jennifer looked at Nick and then gave up the struggle. "Okay, tomorrow, we're going to celebrate all three birthdays because we're starting off as a new family. But normally, you don't get gifts just because your sister is having a birthday!" Jennifer was smiling the entire time she spoke.

"Good decision, Jen. We're going to have a lot of fun tomorrow."

"Oh, I'll need to go shopping!"

"After you take my portrait, I'll take care of the girls so you can go."

"Thank you, Nick. That would be great."

But not as great as tomorrow would be, Nick thought, judging from Annie's megawatt smile. Regardless of what presents she got tomorrow, the little girl had already received the best one—Jennifer Carpenter for a mother.

Chapter Seven

Jennifer had intended to put the girls down for their quiet time, but they all pleaded to watch her take Nick's picture. She agreed reluctantly, but once they were in her home studio, she was glad she'd let the girls watch.

It was better not to be alone with Nick.

Not that she had objected to his kiss. It was pleasant. Pleasant? Asked an inner voice. More like world-shattering. Either way, she'd do well not to repeat it. Nor think about it, she reminded herself as the room suddenly turned warm.

Instead, she went into professional mode. "Which outfit shall we use first?" she asked.

"It doesn't really matter."

After thinking a moment, she said, "Let's try a couple in your sports shirt. That way I can check the lights and film to be sure I have everything working."

"Whatever you say, Jen. You're the expert."

After several minutes of fussing with her equipment,

she looked through the lens at him. "Straighten your back and look toward the light on the right."

He did as she asked and she took several shots. Then she asked him to look over his shoulder. When she repositioned him, he asked, "What do you think?"

"I think the camera loves you."

"Is that a bad thing?" he asked, with a wry grin.

"Of course not." After a couple more pictures, she said, "Go put on your shirt and tie and jacket. We'll take some formal pictures first."

He took his clothes and went into the hall bathroom. When he emerged a couple of minutes later, he had tucked the crisp white shirt into his jeans, tied the tie around his neck and shrugged into the suit jacket. With his midnight hair, the navy-blue pinstripe provided a dark background against which his light eyes glittered.

Jennifer drew in a sharp breath. From the waist up, he looked like the head of a Fortune 500 company. The jeans he wore reminded her he wasn't. She felt sure the portrait would be impressive, which would be good for her. It was easy to make a man like Nick look good. All she had to do was point the camera and click.

Which made her work even harder.

While she was taking the pictures, she talked to him, a technique she'd used with the girls, too. It tended to make the subject relax a little.

"Will your sisters come visit you here? I'd like to meet them."

"I hope they will at Christmas. I'm not sure before then. They're all busy with their own lives."

"Of course. Will your girlfriend visit?"

"No girlfriend. At least not now."

"Ah. But you've had one recently?"

"I was engaged once."

"Turn to face me. What happened to her?"

"She didn't like the idea of settling down. And, like your mother, she didn't have a lot of respect for the job I did."

Jennifer raised shocked eyes to stare at him. "I'm sorry. I know how that feels. Mother thinks I'm wasting my time taking photos."

"She's wrong, if the picture you took of the girls is any indication. But I haven't noticed any patrons on your doorstep. Have you not had any work for a while?"

"I canceled what appointments I had for a couple of weeks because I figured I needed time with the girls more than I needed the work. After all, my picture of the girls will be hung in a gallery for the foster program, along with my name and business card. I figured by the time that happened, I'd have established a routine with the girls and have reassured them."

"That picture should get you a lot of clients."

"Thank you. I love that picture, too."

Halfway through the session he'd changed into a sweater, pulled on over his shirt without a tie, which she discovered made him look even more delicious. She asked, "Exactly what is this picture for?"

"Um, to make people want to—to get to know me."

"You're not going to use it for online dating, are you?" she asked suddenly. It hadn't occurred to her that he would even consider such a thing.

"No! Definitely not!"

"Oh, um, good. I was wondering if we should change the background. That's why I asked."

"To what?"

"I have a background that looks like a study. You know, books on a shelf. I think it would look good."

"Yeah, I'd like that."

Jennifer changed the background with Nick's help. She turned to him and in the cramped quarters was no more than a breath away. "Thanks. You made it a lot easier."

"Call me anytime," he offered with a smile.

The urge to capture that smile on film filled her. "Sit down and keep smiling like that."

"Like what?"

"I don't know, but think whatever you were thinking when you smiled at me."

Nick had no problem reproducing it, and the camera loved it. She snapped several pictures. Then she brought in what looked like the edge of a desk for him to sit on.

"Oh, yes," she muttered as she took several pictures of him in that pose.

"Mommy, we're going to go look at our picture books," Steffi said a few minutes later.

"Okay, honey," Jennifer muttered as she continued to look through the lens.

Half an hour later, she said, "Okay, I think I've taken every pose I can think of. Is there anything else you'd like?"

"Nope. I'll admit this is more tiring than I would've thought. I'm ready to call it quits."

"Okay. I've got some brownies for you and the girls to— Where did the girls go?"

Nick smiled. "They went to their room half an hour ago."

Jennifer could feel her cheeks heating up. "Oh. Sorry. I get carried away when I photograph someone. I'm afraid I go into my own little world."

"That just means you're doing what you're meant to do."

"Do you think so?"

"Yeah. But I'll know better when I see your work," he teased. "Seriously, I have no doubt that you're doing the right thing. It's just fortunate that you had some help from your grandmother. It's hard to get started in a creative kind of work and still support a family."

"Yes, I know."

"Now, where are those brownies? I'm starving."

With a smile, she said, "Follow me." She stopped by the girls' bedroom to see if they wanted brownies, too, then all five of them went to the kitchen. Jennifer set a plate of brownies on the table and provided everyone with a small plate and a glass of lemonade.

"Heaven," Nick said slowly after he took a bite.

"You love chocolate, too?" she asked with a smile.

"You bet. And I think they've proved that it's good for you."

"Well, in moderation, yes. Molière said moderation is the key to a healthy life."

"Molière? You're quoting a French playwright over brownies?"

"Ah, so you've heard of him?"

"What's that, Mommy?" Missy asked.

"Oh, we were just talking about…what we think about life."

"Oh." Obviously not a subject that interested her, Jennifer thought. She tried another. "Do you like the brownies?"

All three girls gave them rave reviews.

Nick leaned across the table and whispered, "We'll compare philosophies another time."

Jennifer couldn't believe how much she looked forward to it.

AT FIVE THE NEXT DAY, Nick knocked on Jennifer's door. When she opened it, he asked, "Are we taking the cake and presents with us, or having them here after pizza?"

"I thought we'd do cake and presents here."

"Good. I like that idea. I'll put my presents here, too." He stepped to the side of the door and picked up a large stack of presents.

"Do you think there's a remote possibility you overdid the present thing?" she teased.

"You said the other two girls should get presents, too, didn't you?"

"Yes, but I meant from me."

He shrugged his shoulders. "I just followed along. Besides, I had a great time shopping. And I didn't spend a lot of money."

"Good. I don't want them to get hooked on video games this early in their lives."

"No, those should wait a year or two."

She rolled her eyes. "At least."

"Is that Dad—Nick, I mean?" Missy called as she reached the living room.

"Yes, it is." Nick reached out to hug Missy lightly. "My, don't you look nice."

The other two girls came out also. "Wow, look at you two. Annie, you're the prettiest birthday girl I've seen in ages!"

The little girl smiled and rubbed her peach-colored shirt. "Mommy bought me my outfit today because it's my birthday."

"Well, she did a good job. It looks great on you. And I think your sisters have new clothes, too."

"Yes, we're all birthday girls tonight," Steffi explained with pride.

"That must be why I brought gifts for all of you."

"You did?" Missy asked in excitement.

Annie's eyes were huge as she stared at Nick. "More presents?" she asked, as if that couldn't be possible.

"Yeah, more gifts. Birthdays are special, sweetheart," he said, swinging Annie up into his arms. "So, are you ready for pizza?"

"Yes," all three girls said at once.

"Jen?"

"Yes, I'm ready. I wish I had earplugs to take with me."

Nick offered her a sympathetic smile. "It won't be that bad, since it's the middle of the week."

"I hope you're right."

When they reached Chuck E. Cheese's, they took the girls in and ordered the pizza and Coke for everyone. After they ate, the girls begged to play the games.

Missy found the ball pit and loved it. She dived in and then erupted into the air, sending the balls in every direction. Annie held back, holding Nick's hand tightly. Steffi looked bored.

Nick leaned forward and whispered to Jennifer. "You keep an eye on our little volcano, and I'll see what the other girls want to do."

Steffi found amusement in some video games, and Annie wandered over to Skee-Ball. She asked questions of Nick and gauged her tosses. Nick decided she had an analytical mind. He'd seen her use that mind in putting together the swing set. Here was a child after his own heart.

When they left two hours later, only because of the promise of cake and presents, Nick and Jennifer exchanged tired glances. But they'd also learned a bit about their little charges.

At Jennifer's, she put candles in the cake and brought it into the living room where the three girls were lined up on the sofa, excitedly waiting. As she came in she began singing Happy Birthday to Annie. Nick joined in and then the two other little girls followed suit.

Jennifer set the cake on the coffee table. "Blow out the candles so your wish will come true, Annie," she said, standing back.

Annie looked first at Jennifer and then Nick, as if she didn't know what to do.

"Blow out the candles, Annie," Nick encouraged. "Then we get to eat some cake. Blow hard!"

Annie finally leaned forward and blew.

Jennifer bent down and kissed her cheek. "Now make your wish, honey." She picked up the cake and headed for the kitchen. "I'll be right back with pieces of cake for everyone."

While Jennifer was in the kitchen, Nick said, "Stay here. I've got to go get another piece of your present from my apartment."

With a grin, he excused himself and hurried to his apartment. He hoped Annie would like his choice. He'd thought about a small tool kit, but he decided she was too young for that just yet.

He rolled a large flat circle into the living room just in time for cake.

As soon as Steffi was done, Nick asked, "Ready for your presents, Annie?"

"Yes," Annie said softly.

He moved a pile of presents to the coffee table. "Oh, my, some of these have other names on them. Let's see, there's one for Steffi and one for Missy, too."

Those two clapped their hands. He offered them the presents with their names on them. But the biggest pile was in front of Annie.

"Okay, Annie," Jennifer said. "You go first. Open a present."

Annie picked up a big one from Jennifer. She carefully untaped the paper and folded it back. Her sisters were telling her to rip the paper off, but she did it her own way. The paper parted to reveal a doll that looked a great deal like Annie with silky blond hair and rosy cheeks.

"Oh, she's beautiful!" Annie said in a whisper. "Thank you, Jennifer."

Jennifer helped her open the box and remove the doll. Annie wrapped her arms around her dolly and rocked back and forth.

"All right, Steffi, Missy, you can open your presents, too."

Paper flew everywhere as the other two girls unwrapped their dolls also, which were not quite as large as Annie's.

"Annie, I think those two are from your sisters," Jennifer said, pointing to more gifts.

With awe in her eyes, Annie opened Steffi's present.

Nick didn't know when the girls had had a chance to shop, but the gift from Steffi was a small coin purse that Annie loved. Then, as Jennifer insisted, she opened Missy's present, a puzzle.

Nick's present came next. Annie opened the first big box and pulled out some sticks of wood. "What is this?"

Nick rolled the flat piece of wood closer. "It's part of your puzzle table. We have to attach the legs. Want to help?"

He pulled his toolbox forward and Annie's eyes lit up. "Oh, yes."

Jennifer and the other two, after opening puzzles from Nick, picked up the wrapping paper and took the dirty dishes to the kitchen. By the time they'd done that, Annie and Nick had the legs attached to the table.

He looked at Jennifer. "I thought we could put this in the corner in their bedroom, so they'd have a place to put together puzzles and color."

"That's a very good idea, Nick…if it fits."

"I'll carry it in there," he said, picking up the table. They all followed him. The table fit beautifully in the corner.

"I'll have to get some chairs for them," Jennifer said.

"Uh, I have those, too. They're in my apartment. I didn't know how to wrap them." He left the room and came back a few minutes later with three little chairs and another box, wrapped in birthday paper.

"Here they are, Annie, and here's one more present."

"What is it?" Annie asked.

"Open it and see." He stood back, pleased with the way his gift had worked out.

The last gift was a puzzle, a round one made for adults.

"I think you should take that one back, Nick. It's too difficult for Annie."

"I think she'll like the challenge."

Jennifer frowned at him. "I think I know my girls better than you."

"I've known them almost as long. Annie is very analytical and loves a challenge."

"Can you show me how to do it?" Annie asked softly, interrupting their argument.

"Sure, honey," Nick said, and sat down in one of the little chairs. Opening the box, he turned it over and let the puzzle pieces rain down on the table. "Don't let any of them hit the floor."

Annie's eyes were wide as she looked at the pile of pieces. "How do I do it?"

He showed her to turn the puzzle pieces over and then look for things that go together. He propped the box lid against the wall so she could look at it.

He looked up at Jennifer to find her glaring at him, her arms crossed over her chest.

"What?" he asked.

"Nothing. Girls, you'll get to play with everything tomorrow. Now it's bedtime. Go wash up and brush your teeth. Annie, you, too."

The child reluctantly left the puzzle table and followed her sisters to the bathroom.

"Oh, Annie, tell Nick thank you for your presents," she called.

Annie ran back in the bedroom and threw her arms around his neck. "Thank you, Nick. I love my puzzle table."

He hugged her back. "I'm glad, honey."

He stood after Annie ran back to the bathroom. "Here's your hat, what's the hurry?"

"I don't know what you mean."

"Look, Jennifer, I should've checked with you first, but I'd been in their room, and I thought the table would fit. I didn't have enough time to ask you."

"So you just assumed you could buy them whatever you wanted? That was too expensive!"

"I bet it cost less than that doll you bought her," he said, not liking her rules.

Her cheeks turned red and she looked away from him. "I don't think that's the point. I'm their mother!"

He shook his head. "Sorry. But I don't see how getting Annie a puzzle table is such a great sin!"

"These are my children, not yours. I make the decisions about them!"

"I bet you never learned to share when you were a kid! And things haven't changed now!" He turned around and walked out of the apartment.

Annie and the other girls crept into the bedroom. "Is Nick mad at me?" Annie asked.

"No, sweetheart," Jennifer hurriedly said. Sitting down on the bed, she took Annie in her lap. "We got in a silly adult argument, but he loves you. He loves all of you. We couldn't ask for a better neighbor, could we?"

The girls all agreed. She helped them dress for bed and tucked them in. Adding good-night kisses, she was almost out the door when Annie asked for her dolly to sleep with her. The other girls made the same request.

Jennifer brought their dolls to them, gave them another round of good-night kisses and softly closed the door behind them.

She leaned against their door, feeling very foolish. Could her anger at Nick have been caused by jealousy? Was the price of his gift okay as long as Annie and the others liked her gift better?

She walked into the living room and paced back and forth. What should she do? She owed him an apology, if that were true, but he should've checked with her before he bought a piece of furniture for her place.

Even if it was perfect.

She started to go to the hall to knock on his door and apologize, but her temper hadn't quite cooled. Maybe it would be better to wait until the morning. She could give a more gracious apology, she assured herself.

Ignoring the little voice that jeered her decision, she picked up a book she'd been reading and headed for her bedroom. She'd talk to Nick tomorrow.

Chapter Eight

Nick drank his first cup of coffee the next morning, going over his argument with Jennifer. She was right; he should've asked her first about buying a piece of furniture for Annie. He knew that. Maybe he should apologize.

On his second cup of coffee, he got stubborn. She was the one who picked the fight. *She* should apologize!

To avoid making a decision, he turned to his computer. He hadn't really gotten down to serious work since his move. He checked his e-mail first. Finding an e-mail from his agent, he realized he hadn't called and given him his new number, despite his promises. Immediately he picked up the phone.

"Hey, Jim, it's Nick."

"I've been waiting for your call. The publisher wanted to know how your book is coming. And the producers who bought your first book are interested in seeing it as soon as you've finished it. They might be interested in picking up the film option."

"That's great, Jim, but I've been settling in. I haven't had time to get much done."

"You have to strike while the iron is hot, Nick. You know that."

"I'm sure I'll have a draft done by the end of September. Will that be soon enough?"

"I'll call them and get back to you."

"Thanks."

After hanging up the phone, Nick reread his proposal and found himself getting lost in the story he was creating. He began drafting the next chapter, and had no idea of the passage of time, getting lost in the action thriller.

When he heard a knock on his door, he was brought back to reality. Jennifer! Jumping up, he hurried to the front door and swung it open.

The woman at his threshold was attractive, but she wasn't Jennifer.

"Yes?" he said.

"Hi, my name is April. I'm one of your neighbors from upstairs. Jennifer said you'd moved in while we were out of town, and I just wanted to introduce myself."

"I'm Nick." He shook her hand. "It's nice of you to stop by, April."

"May I come in? So we can get to know each other a little better?"

"Uh, sure, come in. Would you like a cup of coffee?"

"Oh, that's so sweet of you. Yes, I would."

He went to the kitchen and poured two cups of coffee and brought them back into the living room.

April looked around. "Did you buy Grace's furniture? I'm sure this is the sofa she had."

"No, not really. She sublet the apartment to me because I'm her nephew."

"I see. Where'd she move to?"

"She's had some problems and gone to an assisted-living apartment."

"I'm so sorry to hear that."

He smiled and nodded. Hoping to keep the visit short so he could get back to work, he didn't ask any questions. After a couple of minutes, without having touched her coffee, April stood up to go.

He followed her to the door.

"Remember, I'm just upstairs. If you get…lonely, let me know."

"Thanks, April, I will."

After he closed the door on the flight attendant, he returned to his computer.

Not half an hour later, there was another knock. This was sure to be Jennifer.

He hurried to the door.

An attractive brunette stood there, a smile on her face and a plate in her hand.

"Hi, I'm Rachel. I'm one of your neighbors upstairs. I wanted to welcome you to our building." She offered him the plate of homemade cookies.

"That's very thoughtful of you, Rachel. Won't you come in?"

He poured more coffee for Rachel and shared some

cookies with her as he explained about being Grace's nephew. Rachel asked what he did for a living and he told her he was a teacher.

Would he ever get over hearing Jim Barnes's voice inside his head, telling him not to tell anyone he was a writer? "As soon as they hear your book is being made into a major motion picture, people will assume you're rich. Women will be throwing themselves at you. Believe me, it's more trouble than it's worth. Guard your secret as long as you can." Hence, Nick was still a teacher.

"Oh, that's great," Rachel effused. "I read once that teachers shape the future. That's a big responsibility."

He smiled at her, but he realized she didn't know much about teaching.

After fifteen minutes, she stood and he followed her to the door. At least he got some cookies out of this visit.

He returned to his computer…till another knock sounded at his door.

If this wasn't Jennifer—

He swung open the door to a third stranger, another blonde, this time, but definitely not Jennifer.

The young woman seemed out of breath. "Hi, I'm Amy."

"Let me guess. You live upstairs?"

"Yes," she said with a giggle. "I would've come with Rachel or April, but I had some things I had to do first. Sorry, are we driving you crazy?"

He liked her sense of humor. "Not yet. I appreciate your friendliness."

After her brief visit and yet another knock on his door five minutes later, Nick was ready to call a halt to all the friendliness. He went to the door with a frown on his face.

"Look, I'm—" He pulled his statement to an abrupt halt because this time it was Jennifer.

"I'm sorry to interrupt whatever you're doing, but I wanted to apologize for last night," she said, her cheeks red.

"Come on in. I need to apologize, too. I made some rude remarks to you."

"I—I can't. The girls— I mean, they're working on their puzzles, but I don't like to leave them alone."

"Of course. Look, I was angry and I said things I shouldn't have said. I hope you'll forgive me."

"I believe I was rude first. I'm sorry. All this parenting stuff is new to me. I appreciate all you've done for the girls. You've made them feel more settled."

Nick relaxed against the doorjamb. "That's very generous of you, Jen. How about we kiss and make up?"

She stared at him, her eyes wide. "I don't think—"

He didn't wait for her agreement. He leaned forward and kissed those delectable lips again—finally.

For a few seconds, she participated in the kiss. Then she jerked away. "No! No, we need to stop doing that."

"Why?"

"Because I'm a mother now and—"

He couldn't resist. He kissed her again. This time he wrapped his arms around her so she couldn't run away.

JENNIFER ENJOYED THE FEEL of Nick's arms around her, his lips on hers. It had been a while since she'd been kissed, a while since she'd dated. She'd been concentrating on her career.

Besides, she hadn't found anyone who seemed to understand her as well as Nick did. He believed in her career and he agreed with her decision to adopt the girls. No one else, especially her mother, backed her on both those endeavors. It meant a lot to her.

But as he took the kiss deeper, she forced herself to pull away. "Nick, I can't do this. As I was trying to say, I'm a mother now, and I have to be responsible."

"Does 'responsible' mean no kissing? Because if that's true, then I vote against responsible." He smiled to encourage her.

She took a step away. "I just— I need to get back to the girls."

"Can you get a baby-sitter for this evening?"

"Yes, but I don't want to. I have to have her tomorrow night for the parenting class."

"Get her for tonight and I'll take you out for a steak dinner. Then I'll baby-sit tomorrow night."

"I don't know... No, I don't think so." By now she'd backed all the way to her door. "I'll talk to you later." She opened the door and disappeared behind it. Then she leaned against the door till she caught her breath. Her heart still beat erratically and her lips still burned from his kisses.

Nick Barry was one potent male.

Shaking her head, she pushed away from the door and walked to the girls' room. They were all sitting at the big table Nick had gotten them. Missy was coloring, under Steffi's eye, while she was putting together a puzzle, one of the easier ones Nick had gotten them.

Annie, on the other hand, was working on the complex puzzle Nick had given her. She wasn't even aware of Jennifer entering the room. Jennifer noted that she had almost finished the outer rim of the puzzle, needing only a couple of pieces to connect the circle.

"You're doing a great job on your puzzle, Annie," Jennifer said.

The other girls insisted she look at their work, too.

"Yes, you are all doing well. We need to remember to thank Nick again for the table. It certainly makes a wonderful area for all three of you."

"Can we go thank him now?" Missy asked, jumping up.

"No, not now. He's busy this morning. We'll thank him later."

Though Missy appeared disappointed, she returned to the table.

"I'm going to go put in some laundry. Do you have all your dirty clothes in the laundry basket in the bathroom?"

Steffi and Annie both assured her they did, but Missy jumped up again and ran to put some of her clothes in the basket.

While she was doing that, Jennifer stripped the girls' beds of their sheets.

Once she got the laundry going, she headed for the kitchen to start lunch. While she prepared sandwiches for the four of them, she debated whether to hire someone to come in and help her keep the house tidy. It seemed she had no time to work on her photography now.

The phone rang and it was the photo lab where she'd taken the film of Nick. The pictures were ready, and she couldn't wait any longer to see how they turned out. She immediately put the sandwiches into the refrigerator and gathered up the girls.

"Can Nick go with us?" Missy asked.

"No, sweetie, I want to see the pictures before I show them to Nick. They may not have turned out well."

The woman at the lab allayed her fears. "I think these are the best pictures you've taken, Jennifer."

"Really, Edith? Oh, I hope so. I had a good subject."

"Yeah, I did notice that. He's a handsome devil." She grinned at Jennifer as she handed over the envelope.

"An understatement, for sure." Jennifer wanted to tear into the envelope immediately, but she waited until they were once again in her vehicle.

"Oh, my," she muttered to herself as she went through the photos. Too bad these pictures were going to be used for his résumé and not for a wider distribution. They were some of her best work. She'd use them for her portfolio.

She put them back in the envelope and drove home.

Once there, she put the photos out on the coffee table. "Don't touch the photos, girls. Just look at them. Then you can tell me which one is your favorite."

All four females studied the photos. Finally, Missy said, "I like all of them, Mommy."

"Me, too," Annie said softly.

Steffi pointed out five that she liked best.

With a sigh, Jennifer said, "I agree with you, Steffi. Those are my favorites, too. Let me go knock on Nick's door and have him come look at them."

Nick was frowning when he opened the door.

"I'm sorry to bother you again," Jennifer began.

"Not a problem," he assured her with a smile.

"We've got the proofs back of the pictures I took of you. Do you want to come look at them?"

"Yeah, I do. I didn't know you'd get them back so soon." He followed her across the hall.

He looked at all the photos she'd taken of him. Finally, he selected one of the pictures in which he was wearing the sweater and posing in front of the book-shelves. The one when he was thinking of Jennifer. She'd asked him to replicate his smile, and it hadn't been a problem. All he had to do was think of kissing her.

"You did a great job, Jen. They're all good. But this is the one I like best."

"All right. How many copies do you need?"

"Uh, five should do it."

"Okay. It'll take a few days to get them ready."

"Great." He turned to the girls. "Are you all okay with this picture?" he asked.

They agreed enthusiastically.

"How about I take you all to lunch to celebrate?"

Jennifer knew the girls' answer before they exploded with excitement. She thought about the half-made sandwiches in the fridge, but in the end she agreed to go out to lunch with Nick.

"THIS IS FUN," Missy said with a big grin when they'd sat down with their meals. "I like eating out."

"But your Mommy is a really good cook," Nick pointed out.

"Yeah, especially when she makes us cookies."

Nick shared a smile with Jennifer. "Yeah, but you can't live on just cookies."

"Why not?" Missy asked.

"Because you need a balanced diet. You know, green things, red things, yellow things. See, you're eating them now."

Missy frowned. "Where?"

"On your burger, the tomatoes are red, lettuce is green, and the cheese is yellow."

"Oh, that's okay, then. I like those things." Missy obviously approved.

"Um, Nick, all of us wanted to thank you again for the puzzle table," Jennifer said. "We're really enjoying it. Right, girls?"

They all nodded.

"I'm glad. How's the puzzle coming, Annie?"

"I've finished the circle. Now I have to fit the rest of it together."

"Good for you."

Softly, Jennifer said, "I was wrong about that, too, Nick. You understood Annie better than I do."

"That's because we share a lot of the same things, Annie and I. I like to put things together, too. It fills me with a sense of accomplishment."

"Yes, and I'm going to remember that about Annie. I think she's really blossomed since I took her in."

"That's because she's gone from abuse to the love you've shown them. You're a great mom, Jen, even though you don't have much experience. I just think you shouldn't forget that you need some attention, too."

"What are you talking about?"

Nick smiled at her. "A mom can't do everything for the kids and forget that she needs fun and time, too."

She stiffened. "I know that. I've decided to hire a housekeeper to come at least once a week."

"Good. But two days might be better. Then you'll be able to get out on your own without the girls."

"I don't need to do that."

"Well, think about it. And if you find someone good, I could use a housekeeper once a week, too."

She looked at him, surprised. "Can you— I mean, a good housekeeper will cost a hundred dollars for a full day."

"I know."

"All right. I'll see what I can find." She took a bite of her lunch. "You know, I was thinking, are you sure you only need five copies of your portrait? If you're applying to a lot of different school districts, you may need more than that."

"Well, maybe ten copies. What will that run me?"

"Oh, twenty-five dollars."

"Come on, Jen, I'm serious."

Jennifer looked at the girls quickly. They were seated in a round booth and the girls were chatting among themselves. She leaned toward Nick. "I told you you'd only have to pay for the paper. My services were free."

"Even your film? I have to pay for the film, too. And I know photo paper is more expensive than that."

"Nick, just pay what I said and quit complaining. You're taking us out for lunch and I intend to let you pay. Turn-about, fair play."

"Fine. I'll just owe you five more lunches!"

She was about to object but he cut her off. "How are you going to make your name by giving away your work?"

"I'm hoping people will look at your photos and decide I can do a good job."

"So the more I show my picture, the better for you?"

"Yes, of course."

"I'll see what I can do."

She frowned. Did he think using his photo on

résumés for a teaching job would bring her a lot of notoriety? She just shook her head.

"By the way, I think you told the ladies upstairs about me. They each came to visit me this morning, one at a time." He gave her a lopsided smile. "Thanks a lot."

"Oh. I'm sorry, but I thought— You needed to meet the rest of your neighbors."

"But aren't there three more?"

"Well, yes, but they won't be back for several more days."

"Well, there's no rush."

She wiped her lips with her napkin. "It'll give you more, uh, friends to do things with."

"I'm not going to have much time to play. I'm…writing a lot this summer."

"What are you writing?"

Her question seemed to be difficult to answer. He seemed to study his reply before speaking. Finally he said, "I'm writing a novel."

"Writing a novel? I thought you were a teacher."

"I am. But I'm taking a break from teaching to write for a while." He looked away and said, "Sorry I didn't tell you, but I'm still a little skeptical about it."

"And you need a picture? Before you even sell the book?"

He cleared his throat. "Actually, I've already got a contract for it."

"What kind of book?"

"An action thriller. But I'll need a picture for the back cover—and it will give you some exposure, too."

"That's great. That's one of the reasons I did The Heart Gallery with the girls. Maybe I should pay you to let me take your picture."

"Don't be ridiculous. I'm no Stephen King."

"I should hope not! I certainly wouldn't want my children to spend time with a horror writer!"

"Then I'm glad I don't write horror." He smiled more easily since the conversation had started.

"Me, too. Is this the first book you've sold?"

"No, actually, I've sold another book, but it won't be out until September."

"Oh, so you'll be famous in September?" she teased.

"Probably not."

"It's okay. I'm still pleased to take your picture." She smiled at him.

The waitress stopped by to be sure they didn't need anything, and he asked for a refill on his soft drink.

Before she could continue their conversation, which she was enjoying, Nick turned to the children and asked if they had favorite books.

Steffi definitely did. Missy didn't know the name of her favorite book, but she insisted on telling the story to Nick, from start to finish. Annie hadn't said anything, so he looked at her next.

"I like Cinderella," she said, looking unsure of how the others would react.

"That's a lovely story, honey," Nick said. "Good choice."

Jennifer made a mental note to rent the movie *Ever After* for Annie, right after she finished her errands this afternoon. She still had to sign the girls up for ballet classes. Not only did she think they'd enjoy it, they'd have the opportunity to make friends before school started. When everyone was done she told Nick her plans.

"Then you'd better get to it." He waved for the waitress and offered his credit card to pay the bill.

Jennifer worried about what kind of debt he was collecting. It was easy to get carried away charging, she knew, and it could trip a person up later.

After they dropped off Nick, she drove to the dance studio where she'd taken ballet as a child.

She introduced the girls to the owners of the school, Mr. George and Mrs. Beverly. Then she enrolled all three girls in the first basic class. They were to start tomorrow morning.

They bought their tights, leotards, ballet shoes and tutus. Annie was fascinated with the tutu. She held hers in her lap all the way home.

"Okay, girls, we've had a busy day. Now, go lie down for an hour and try to go to sleep," Jennifer said.

"I'm not sleepy," Steffi complained.

"Just rest, honey. You don't have to go to sleep."

Once she got the girls down, she fixed herself a glass of iced tea and was going to sit down and relax, when there was a knock on her door.

She opened it and found Nick there.

"Hi, come on in. Want a glass of iced tea?"

"Yeah, that'd be great."

He waited until she went to the kitchen and returned with an iced tea for him. Then he sat down on the sofa.

"Uh, Jennifer, I wanted to tell you…well, I lied to you this afternoon."

Chapter Nine

Nick waited for her reaction. He'd decided it was time to come clean about his career. Jim Barnes be damned.

Jennifer stared at him, as if she couldn't believe his words.

"Take a drink of iced tea," he suggested.

Instead, she set her glass down on the coffee table. "No, I want to know what you're talking about."

"I told you I'd sold another book before this one."

That apparently wasn't what she expected. "But you haven't?"

"Yes, I have."

"Then what is it you're lying about?"

"My first book was picked up by a producer in Hollywood."

"You're kidding!"

He shrugged. "I got lucky."

"And that means you don't have to teach again?"

"Only because when I sold my book, someone in

Hollywood looked at it and bought it for a movie. They're filming it right now."

"Really?" she exclaimed, her eyes big, reminding him of Annie.

He rubbed the back of his neck, feeling uncomfortable.

"They are really making a movie from your book and they'll show it in real theaters?"

"Yeah."

Jennifer stood and began pacing the room. "So are they buying your next book, too?"

"Hopefully. I've got to finish it first."

She continued to stare at him. He could only describe her look as horror-stricken. But then he'd been accused of being overly dramatic.

"And you've let us interfere with your work? Oh, no, Nick, I'm so sorry!"

"Jen, it's not that big a deal. I hadn't gotten started until this morning. And I'm used to interruptions."

"Maybe, but I shouldn't have let you take so much time, going shopping with us, putting together the swing set. You'll be famous and— Your photo is for the book jacket of your first book, the one they're making into a movie?" she suddenly demanded, her face lighting up.

Nick laughed. "Not famous, but yes, the photo will be used on the book jacket. That's why I thought I should be honest with you."

"Do you realize how much exposure that will give

me?" Jennifer sat back down on the sofa. "Oh, my. My first photo that will go all over the world!"

"Well, yeah, but—"

"You don't understand how important this is. Let's see, we'll need some eight-by-ten glossies in black and white and in color. What does your publisher want?"

"We can just send them the pictures you're making copies of."

"Yes, of course. I can have them ready in a couple of days. Will that be soon enough?"

"Yes, of course, Jen. Look, it's not that big a deal. I just felt bad leading you on, and you worrying about whether or not I could make it. I mean, I'm still getting my teacher's salary until September, anyway. But I wanted you to know that I'm all right."

"Well, thank you, and I promise we won't take up your time like we've been doing."

"No! I don't want you to stay away. I'll get lonesome over there all by myself."

"But you'll be writing."

"Not all the time. I'll still have time for the girls…and you."

"But I may become busy once people see my photo on the back of your book." She flashed him a smile. "I might be in demand."

"I hope so. But I'll help with the girls whenever you need me. Okay?"

"Yes, but I'll manage."

"But, Jen—"

She was urging him toward the door. "I know you want to get back to your writing. Thanks for telling me."

And suddenly Nick found himself out in the hall. Damn it, this wasn't what he wanted! He just didn't like lying to her!

But now she wouldn't include him in things she did with the girls. They would tiptoe past his apartment, worrying about disturbing him. And he'd shrivel up in his apartment, without a new thought in his head.

Okay, so maybe he *was* being overly dramatic. Jennifer would get over the idea that she shouldn't bother him. Wouldn't she?

JENNIFER EXPLAINED TO HER girls over dinner that Nick was writing a book and would be too busy to do things with them. They weren't happy, but their enthusiasm returned when she told them about her photo.

Annie's eyes got big. "He's writing a book? Can we read it?"

"I don't think it's a children's book, but we'll buy a copy when it comes out. And you know what? One of the pictures I took of him will be on the back of his book!"

"Is that good?" Steffi asked.

Ever the analytical one, Annie offered, "Maybe because people will look at it and decide they want you to take their pictures."

Steffi chimed in. "That would be a good idea because you make great pictures. Look at what you did for us."

Jennifer felt emotion tighten her throat. What had she ever done to deserve these girls? "Thanks, honey," she managed to say.

"Mommy, after dinner, can we go out and play with Blondie? She's getting lonesome in the backyard by herself."

"I guess so, Missy. You'll have a couple of hours after dinner before bedtime and it's staying light until almost nine o'clock. Before you go, I wanted to ask you a question. Would you like to take swimming lessons?"

"But we don't have a swimming pool," Steffi pointed out.

"I know, but there's a place I can take you that does have a pool and someone there will teach you to swim. It's a good thing to learn so you can be prepared for whatever comes along."

"Okay," Steffi agreed.

"How about you two? Are swimming lessons okay?"

Both Annie and Missy agreed.

"Okay, I'll make the arrangements while you're playing with Blondie."

All three girls left the kitchen and Jennifer was deafened by the sound of silence. Funny how before the girls her apartment was always quiet and it never bothered her. In another way, though, she'd always yearned for family—other than her mother. That was why she'd thought about contacting her half brother—an idea that still had appeal. She just didn't have the time now.

She cleared the table and quickly did the dishes, planning to set up some interviews with housekeepers. One who could work for her two days a week and one day for Nick. Not that she was responsible for him, but he'd need someone to clean his apartment. She'd heard writers got involved in their writing and didn't notice the things around them.

Okay, so she was thinking of Nick, not an impersonal "them." She was excited about his future, and her own, she admitted. But she would miss not having Nick around. She already did.

He had shored up her belief that she could be a parent. And he had encouraged her to go to parenting classes. And he'd made her feel that she had backup if she needed it. But now she didn't feel that she could interrupt him.

He might be writing.

Suddenly she felt almost as alone as she did when she didn't have the girls.

NICK FELT ALONE.

He was actually getting some writing done, though, in spite of the worry that Jennifer would shut him out of her little family. He was giving her a little time, hoping that she might miss him.

When a knock disturbed his work, he eagerly hurried to answer it, hoping, dreaming it was Jennifer.

But the vision before him was more like a nightmare. It was Jennifer's mother.

"Where is my daughter?" the haughty woman demanded without any greeting.

"You're knocking on the wrong door. That's her door over there."

"I know that!" the woman spat out. "But she's not there!"

He looked at his watch. "Oh, she's probably at the girls' ballet class."

"She put them in ballet class? That's ridiculous! They don't know anything about ballet."

"That would be the reason for the classes, wouldn't it?" He leaned against the door, finding this interruption very interesting.

"When will she be home?"

"I don't know, Mrs. Carpenter. I'm not her gatekeeper."

"What a difficult young man!"

He ignored her nasty remark. "Would you like to leave a note for Jen?"

"Jen? Her name is Jennifer. Don't call her Jen!"

He shrugged. "She's never objected."

"Well, I do. It's…common!"

He nearly laughed in her face. "I think that's Jen's decision," he said, intentionally using his pet name for her daughter.

"I need a pen and paper. I'm trying to help Jennifer, but it's hard to do that when I can't even find her."

"Come right this way." Once he led her into his apartment and got her the supplies, she sat down on his sofa and wrote her a note. Then she carefully folded it.

"Please give this to Jennifer when she returns."

"I'll be happy to."

She wagged a finger in his face. "And don't read it!"

Nick just smiled and took the note. Then he escorted the woman out the door. Mrs. Carpenter didn't realize she'd actually done him a favor: she'd given him a reason to contact Jennifer.

But Jennifer didn't come home. Not when ballet should have been over, nor an hour later, or two. Nick began to worry about her and the three little ones. What if they'd had an accident? She would call him, wouldn't she? He began to pace, trying to imagine what they could be doing.

He kept checking his watch. She could be doing any number of things, but he didn't know what. It would be ridiculous to demand her schedule each day, but how could he get any work done if he thought she or the girls were in danger?

When her car finally pulled into the lot, he was outside to let the girls out.

"Daddy!" Missy called out, forgetting herself.

"Hi, sweetheart. Where have y'all been? I thought you'd be here an hour ago."

"We bought swimsuits," Annie said with a big smile.

He ushered all three girls to the sidewalk. "Swimsuits? But we don't have a swimming pool."

"Mommy said we need to learn so we'll be safe around water," Steffi explained.

Jennifer got out of her car and joined them on the

sidewalk. "What are you doing out here, Nick? You should be inside writing!"

"Jen, I can't write all the time. I need to be around other people, do things, not stay locked up in my apartment."

"You do? Are you sure?"

He rolled his eyes. "Yes, I'm sure."

"But you didn't say anything about that."

"You didn't give me a chance. You just hustled me out of your apartment before I could even explain."

"I'm sorry." She looked around, puzzled. "Have you been waiting for us to return just so you can tell me that?"

"Uh, no. I had a message to give you."

"A message? From whom?"

"Your mother. She came in and wrote you a note when she couldn't find you at home. That seemed to upset her."

"Yes, she expects everyone to be at her beck and call," Jennifer said, a touch of sarcasm in her voice. "So where's the all-important message?"

"It's inside. I'll get it and bring it to your apartment."

"Okay. I'm fixing sandwiches for lunch. Have you eaten?"

"No, but you don't need—"

"It's not a problem to fix an extra sandwich, Nick, and the girls have been complaining about not seeing you. Unless you need to get back to the computer, we'd love to have you join us."

"Then I'll gladly accept."

He rejoined them in Jen's kitchen, note in hand. "Here it is, Jen."

She put down the food she was getting out for lunch and opened the note. After reading it, she crumpled the paper and threw it in the trash and continued making lunch.

"Is everything all right?" he asked.

"Did you read it?"

"No. It wasn't written to me."

"You can be glad it wasn't written to you." She began putting the sandwiches together.

"Why?"

"Because it's not her showing concern or offering to be a part of my new family. It's an attempt to set me up with a man she thinks is perfect for me. As long as I get rid of—of complications," she said, after a quick look at the girls.

"She's still playing that old song?" Nick asked.

"She never changes."

"What are you talking about?" Steffi asked.

"Nothing that needs to concern you, sweetie," Jennifer said. "Have you told Nick about your ballet class?"

"Was it fun, Steffi?" Nick asked.

"Yeah, we learned some steps. Want me to show you?"

"Yes, of course."

"Me, too," Missy said, jumping down from her chair. Both girls moved their feet to first position.

"Well done. You're on your way, aren't you?"

"Yes. We're going twice a week," Steffi told him.

"I want to show Nick my swimsuit," Annie said, looking at Jennifer for approval.

"You can show him, but don't try them on now. Lunch is almost ready."

"Come on, Nick," Annie said, taking his hand.

Nick followed Annie back to the living room where they'd left some packages. She dug through a big sack and pulled out a bright red swimsuit with blue, green and yellow stripes across the chest.

"My, that's very pretty, Annie. I wouldn't have thought you'd choose those colors."

"Mommy said we needed bright colors so someone could see us in the water."

"That's good thinking. Once you learn to swim, maybe we'll find a place with a swimming pool where you can show me. When do you start swimming lessons?"

"In the morning. We're going to swim on the days we don't go to ballet."

"That's very good. You'll get a lot of exercise."

Missy, who had followed them, added, "And we play with Blondie every day, too."

"Where is Blondie?"

"In the backyard. She has her own doghouse and everything."

"She has her doghouse and you have your swing set. Are you swinging a lot?"

Annie nodded. "Yep."

"I like to climb up on the slide," Missy said. "But Steffi makes me slide down."

When Jennifer called, they all went to the table and enjoyed a good lunch together. Afterward, Jennifer sent the girls to their room to rest.

"You've done a lot since I was over here," Nick commented.

"Not really. I just arranged swimming lessons for the girls."

"And got a doghouse for Blondie."

"I only bought one and had it delivered."

"I just assumed Blondie would be an inside dog."

"She can come in, but the girls like to go outside and play with her."

"Okay," he said as he gathered up the dishes and carried them to her at the sink.

"Oh, and I'm interviewing a lady to do the housekeeping."

"Should I sit in on the interview?"

"You can if you want. I'm going to hire her for all four apartments. You'll each have her for one day a week and I'll have her for two days. It will be a hundred dollars for each day."

"You talked to the others and they agreed?"

"Yes. Have you changed your mind?"

"No, not at all."

The doorbell rang and Jennifer looked at her watch. "She's a little early," she said as she hurried to the door.

Nick wiped off the table before he joined Jennifer

in the living room. But it wasn't the housekeeper inter-viewee that was talking to Jennifer. It was her mother.

"Did you give her the note?" Mrs. Carpenter de-manded as he strolled in.

"Sure did."

"Jennifer, I thought I made it plain in the letter that you need to get rid of those children!"

"Mother, you have no right to make that kind of a demand. I am an adult and I won't have you upsetting my children."

"They aren't your children," her mother pointed out.

"For the last time, Mother, yes, they are. Those girls are mine and nothing you can do will change that."

As if she hadn't heard Jennifer, the woman contin-ued her demands. "Get rid of them, Jennifer, or I'll never speak to you again."

"Fine. It makes—" Just then she noticed Steffi in the room. "Steffi? What's wrong?"

The little girl turned and ran back down the hall.

"Go away, Mother! I've got to go take care of my children!"

Jennifer ran from the room. Nick remained, glaring at the woman in front of him. How could anyone be so cold?

"You're staring, young man!"

"Yeah, I am. I can't believe that you would shut yourself off from the only daughter you have just because she doesn't do exactly what you want her to do."

"You know nothing about anything. Jennifer is a

blueblood who can marry whomever she wants. Unless she sabotages her life by getting all sentimental over someone else's children!"

"I think you'd better leave before Jennifer comes back. She's not going to be happy with you for upsetting the girls."

"You have no right to throw me out of my daughter's house."

"No, but *I* do," Jennifer said as she walked into the room. "And I don't want you to come back here unless you're willing to accept my choices in life."

"Really, Jennifer, I see no need for such rudeness," the woman said, her nose in the air.

"Those are my terms, Mother. Take them or leave them. But they are not negotiable. I don't want you doing any more damage to my children."

"Oh!" The woman stamped her foot in frustration and then turned to leave. Before she opened the door she said, "Call me if you come to your senses."

"Goodbye, Mother."

After the door closed behind the woman, Jennifer slumped down onto the sofa.

"Are the girls all right?" Nick asked.

"Yes, I think so. I tried to reassure them that I love them and they're not going to be taken from me."

"Did they believe you?"

"I hope so."

"Mind if I go say goodbye?"

"Of course not. I'm going to finish cleaning the kitchen."

Nick went to the girls' room and knocked softly on the door. Then he opened it.

All three girls were sitting on the lower bed, crying.

Chapter Ten

Nick stepped into the room. "What's wrong, girls?"

"You know," Steffi said. "Mommy's mother wants us to go away."

Nick sat down beside her and carefully wiped the tears away. "That's true, but Jennifer doesn't want that."

"But it's not fair for her to lose her mommy," Annie said. "We know how hard that is. Steffi says we should run away so Jennifer's mommy will come back."

"That's very giving of you, Annie, but it would be terrible for Jennifer. You know, I lost my mother, too, and I know how hard it is. But Jennifer is all grown up and she can decide whether she wants her mommy in her life. You know, Jennifer loves you three very much."

"She does?" Steffi asked.

"She does. She's planning on being your mommy for the rest of her life. If you leave, she'll be all alone. She would cry a lot."

"Then we can't leave," Missy said with a sniff. "I don't want Jennifer to cry."

Annie looked at Nick. "Does that mean we get to stay? We won't have to run away?"

Before Nick could hug the little girl and assure her she shouldn't run away, Jennifer came in.

"What's going on?"

Nick gave her a reassuring smile. "I'm explaining to the girls that they shouldn't run away because you would miss them."

Jennifer almost fell over. "What? Of course I would miss them." She turned to the girls. "Why would you even think about running away?"

"So your mommy won't be mad at you," Steffi explained.

Jennifer closed her eyes for a minute. Then she sank onto the mattress with the rest of them. "Steffi, my mother is not— She's not like your mommy. She doesn't really care what happens to me if I don't do exactly what she says. But I'm an adult, and I get to make choices about my life. When you grow up, you'll get to make choices about your life. I always want you to love me, but I know you'll make the decisions. That's the way life is. But my mother doesn't play by the rules."

"What does that mean?" Missy asked.

"It's too hard to explain, sweetheart, but don't run away. I would miss you so much. Okay?"

"We don't want to," Annie said, "but we want you to be happy."

"I am, as long as I have you three. We're a family."

Nick leaned toward the girls. "And, as the, uh, neighbor of this family, I expect to be notified before you do anything that risky. Got it?" The girls nodded. "Then how about a group hug? That's what we always did in my house."

The girls threw themselves at both Jennifer and Nick, giving them big hugs and wet kisses. Eventually, they began to giggle, which brought joyful laughter to Jennifer. Nick laughed, too, glad to bring a happy ending to such a deserving family.

To celebrate, he kissed Jennifer, right there in front of the girls. Then he walked to the door. "I'll see you later."

"I LIKE NICK," MISSY SAID with a big smile. "And I think he likes you, too."

"Yes, we all like Nick," Jennifer said hurriedly, willing away the blush from her cheeks. "But—but let's talk about you. You don't have to tell Nick when you're upset. You should tell me. I'll fix it if I can. Okay?"

Once she had the assurances from her three charges, she told them to lie down and rest before they went out to play with Blondie.

Jennifer went to her own bedroom, where she sank down on the bed. Warnings ping-ponged in her brain. Warnings to back off from Nick. He was getting too involved with her and the girls, but his career path wouldn't lead to domesticity. If they were making a film from his book, he was destined for bigger things. He'd probably be moving to Hollywood.

That wasn't a place for her or her daughters. She didn't want any of them to have their hearts broken by Nick's departure. And she was already falling in love with him. Just a little bit.

The doorbell rang and this time she was sure it was the housekeeping interview. She'd called an agency and they said they had a perfect candidate who loved kids.

Jennifer opened the door and invited in a smiling, middle-aged woman.

Her smile was a good start.

They discussed the setup. The only one that caused concern was the six stewardesses in one apartment, but Jennifer reassured her about the group. When they were both satisfied with the interview, Jennifer went to the girls' room and invited them to come meet the lady who would be taking care of the apartment.

They lined up in front of the woman, and she bubbled over with excitement. "They are so darling!"

"Girls, this is Mrs. Carroll. She will come clean two days a week. You must be sure to have your dirty clothes in the laundry basket before she comes and all your toys put away. Okay?"

They nodded. Then Missy leaned close to Mrs. Carroll. "I'm the messiest one, but I'll try really hard to put my dirty clothes in the basket."

"Good. And I'll help you," she said, stifling a smile.

"I'm very pleased, Mrs. Carroll," Jennifer said. "You'll start here on Monday and I'll make a schedule for the other apartments."

Jennifer escorted the woman out. When she turned around, she nearly bumped into Missy.

"Does that mean we need to tell Nick?" Missy asked.

"Well, yes, but I'll just call him."

"But I want to ask him to come out and play."

"No! No, we can't do that, sweetie. He's busy."

"Can't we just ask?"

"Not today. Go play with Blondie. I think she misses you."

That convinced Missy, who ran for the backyard.

WHEN THE WEEKEND CAME, Nick wanted to take a break. He'd been writing steadily for several days. He strolled across the hall and knocked on Jennifer's door.

There was no answer. With a frown he returned to his apartment and went to the back bedroom, which had a view of the backyard. He didn't see anyone outside.

Probably because it was too hot. Why was he looking for Jennifer and her girls, anyway? Getting back to work had reminded him of the kind of life he'd planned for himself here in Dallas. He was going to be alone, productive, focused, not lose his chance at the limelight.

He was attracted to Jennifer. Hell, he was attracted to all of them. But did he want the difficulty of a family? He thought about that for a minute. Why not? He wanted a family…one day.

He moved back to the front of his apartment to see if Jennifer's car was in the parking lot. For right now, he wanted to see her and the girls.

No, it was gone. Why hadn't he heard them leaving? He stuffed his hands in his pockets and began pacing the floor, which made him think he was a lot like Jennifer's mother.

But he certainly wasn't going to lay down ultimatums.

When his phone rang, he was surprised to hear his agent's voice. "Jim, what are you doing calling on a Saturday?"

"You're not going to believe this, Nick. I got an emergency phone call from Hollywood. They're having trouble adapting a scene to film. Several of their hotshot writers have tried, but they aren't satisfied with the results. They thought they'd give you a chance."

Nick could hardly believe his ears. Hollywood wanted his help? "What scene?"

"I have no idea. They want you to fly out right away."

"Fly out? To Hollywood?"

"Yes. They'll pay for your expenses. They've got a ticket waiting for you. Just go check in." He gave Nick the flight information.

"I won't have to be there very long, will I?"

"Why not? You're single. Hollywood will be great for you."

"Are they talking a couple of days or a week?"

"I have no idea." Jim hesitated, then he asked, "Nick, are you okay?"

"Yeah, I'm fine. I'll get out to Hollywood."

"Here's the number to call before you board your flight. That way someone will pick you up."

"Right. Thanks, Jim."

Nick hung up the phone and stared at it for several seconds without moving. Here was the opportunity he thought he wanted. Strange, his heart wasn't racing. He was thinking about leaving Jennifer and her girls.

He shook his head as if to banish the thoughts and went to his bedroom to pack.

When that was done, he took out some paper to write Jen a note. That wasn't how he wanted to leave, but he had to tell her what was going on.

He was halfway through his note when he heard some noise in the hallway. He sprang to his feet and threw open his door.

"Did we disturb you?" Jennifer asked as she urged her children inside her apartment.

"I've been waiting for you."

"You have?"

"Yeah. I've got to leave."

"Where are you going?" Missy asked, stepping out into the hall.

"I have to go to California," he said, squatting down beside Missy. "Will you give me a goodbye hug?"

"Yes," Missy agreed, throwing her arms around his neck.

Annie and Steffi followed Missy. In the meantime, Missy was asking when he would be coming home.

"I'm not planning on being gone longer than a week. But I won't know how long until I get there."

"We'll miss you," Annie said.

"I'll miss all of you, too, but I'll be back. Now, I need to talk to your mommy for just a minute, okay?"

Jennifer, who had backed up to her apartment door, opened it and told the girls to go wash up for lunch.

She stood there, not moving toward him. He crossed the distance between them in two strides. "I should've given you all this information before, but here are my sisters' names and numbers…just in case something goes wrong."

"Are you sure you'll be coming back?" she asked, staring at the paper he'd given her.

"What do you mean?"

"You're going to Hollywood. Anything can happen."

"I'm not sure what they have in mind for me, Jennifer. They may need me longer, but I've only packed for a week." He smiled and ran a finger across her cheek. "But I'll be back eventually," he said, leaning just a little closer.

"Okay." Jennifer couldn't think of anything else to say. If she tried, she was afraid she'd say something she shouldn't. But it disturbed her how much his departure upset her. Even though she'd expected it.

"I'll miss you," he muttered, and then kissed her. He took her in his arms and pulled her close, needing to feel her. She opened up to him and deepened the kiss.

She put a finger to his lips. "Don't, Nick. I—I have to go inside. To be with the girls."

"I know. Take care of them until I get back."

"I will. Take care of yourself." She backed into her apartment and closed the door.

Nick stood there for a moment reliving that kiss. Then he went into his apartment to grab his suitcase and called a taxi to take him to the airport. He was on his way to Hollywood!

JENNIFER LEANED AGAINST the door, her eyes closed, thinking about his goodbye kiss. She needed to remember it because she figured once he got to Hollywood, he wouldn't think of her or the girls anymore.

"Mommy?" Missy asked.

"Uh, yes, sweetie?"

"Why do you have your eyes closed?"

"I was just resting a minute. Are you hungry?"

"Yes. But I'm going to miss Nick."

"Yes, sweetie, we all will. But Nick may move to California, so don't plan on him being around all the time."

"But I don't want him to. He's the daddy!"

"No, Missy. I told you he isn't the daddy. He's a neighbor, but that can change, so you mustn't count on him."

Missy fell silent, a sad look on her face, and Jennifer couldn't help but hug her. Then she hurried her into the kitchen.

After lunch she sent the girls to rest. And she went to her own bedroom, taking the piece of paper Nick had given her. She folded it and put it under her jewelry box to keep it safe. She didn't think anything bad would happen.

Except that Nick wouldn't come home.

NICK WANTED TO GO HOME.

He was frustrated. Every time he solved one problem, the people doing the film came up with another. He'd spent three long days putting out fires, and three long nights being taken to one club after another. Each one was filled with beautiful women, some single some not. But his guide, one of the writers, said it didn't matter. They were all available to anyone who had either money or power.

"But I don't have either," Nick said.

"They'll think you have power. They'll think you could get them a job on the set. That's the way to fame and fortune."

Nick shook his head. "Shouldn't we be working instead of partying?"

"We've told the director we need time to work these things out," the other writer said with a grin. He was about twenty-six years old and had lived in Hollywood after getting out of film school at UCLA. He didn't know another way of life existed.

"Hey, Nick, you work too fast. We don't want to overdo it."

Nick thought about Jennifer and the girls and the time he'd spent with them. That time had been so much more fun. So had the time he had been alone and worked on his book. He'd already learned it was important to enjoy the process of the writing as much as the results.

"You know, I need to wind up my work tomorrow and head back home. I've discovered I'm a homebody."

"I should've known you were married. You haven't picked up a woman the entire time you've been here. And you have your own hotel room, paid for!"

Actually he had a suite, in a five-star hotel that was beyond his wildest dreams. Still… "I'm tired of it. I want to go home."

"But you could have a regular job writing here. They like your work."

The director had told him as much yesterday when Nick had shown up on the set with the rewrites. Nick had been thrilled, but his elation waned when Jen wasn't there to share it. The director had clapped him on the back and recommended Nick try his hand at writing screenplays. The Hollywood hotshot was well connected, his reputation having drawn some marquee names to this film.

Nick could hardly believe his ears. This was a break people would kill for and it was being offered to *him*. This was his chance—to make it, to be famous, rich. But why hadn't he jumped at it? It was everything he ever wanted… But no longer.

Now the only dreams that filled his head had four blondes in them. And he couldn't wait to get home to them.

The next day, Nick informed all involved that he was going home after that day. He was amazed how much better he felt after he made his decision. His sleep that last night was so much more peaceful.

"Man you are the cheapest date we've every brought to town," was his guide's last comment to Nick.

"Good. I don't need to run up the costs of making the film. But I need to get back to Dallas."

"You must have one hot lady in Dallas!"

"Yes, I do," Nick said, smiling for almost the first time since his arrival.

"Okay. I'll see what flight I can get you on. I tell you what. I'll get you a first-class ticket. Then you can fly in comfort."

"That's a deal."

When Nick knew what flight he would be on, he called Jennifer. No one answered, so he left a message. "Hey, Jen, girls, I'm getting in at 3:35 this afternoon. How about I take you out to dinner? I've missed you all."

Then he hung up the phone, counting on the girls to persuade Jennifer to accept his invitation.

JENNIFER WAS DRINKING iced tea out on the deck, sitting at a new table with an umbrella to provide some shade. She and Diane were chatting about the girls and the changes in Jennifer's life.

"I think this has been great for you, Jennifer," Diane said. "I've never seen you so happy."

She couldn't help but smile now. "The girls are wonderful. And Nick suggested I take a parenting class that has really helped, too."

"Where is Nick? I haven't seen him lately."

"He…" Nick hadn't told her it was all right to spread the news of his career change and his Hollywood trip, so she kept his confidence. "He had to go out of town."

"Really? I thought he was just lazing around for the summer before he started teaching again."

"I'm not sure what he's doing. He has three sisters. He may be visiting one of them." Then she hurried to change the subject.

"Why are you off today?"

"Oh, I just decided to take a vacation day. The summer has become a drag. I needed a day off."

"That's nice. How'd the housekeeper work out?"

"She's wonderful! Will Nick be back on Friday when she does his apartment?"

"I'm not sure. He thought he'd be gone a full week."

"You know, I took your advice with him." When Jennifer shot her a puzzled look, she explained, "I took him out to dinner as you suggested, though he insisted on paying. We had a nice visit, but…he wasn't interested."

"How do you know?"

"It was easy to tell. I don't need a picture drawn for me. He was polite, but nothing more."

"Well, I—"

"I hear your phone ringing," Diane said.

"It's probably my mother. She calls constantly to tell me how she hates the idea that I'm adopting the girls. She wanted to set me up with some millionaire's son. According to her, no one will want me now. I'm a 'package deal,' as she calls it."

"Maybe your mom could adopt me. I could use that guy!"

Jennifer laughed along with her friend. "Sounds good to me. The next time she calls, I'll accept and you can go in my place."

"Don't you think that would make her mad?"

"Yes, but I don't care. As long as you and the guy hit it off, we don't have a problem."

"Mommy!" Missy called from down below. Jennifer got up and went to the rail. "Yes, Missy?"

"I'm very hot."

Missy looked flushed. Steffi and Annie were on the swings, but Missy had been running all over with Blondie.

"Come up here, sweetie. I think you need to cool down."

She met Missy at the top of the stairs and felt her face. "Oh, my, I think you're running a fever."

She brought Missy back to her chair and sat down, pulling Missy into her lap. She gave her some of her iced tea and then rubbed the cold glass against her cheeks.

After a few minutes, when Missy was still hot, Jennifer decided to call the pediatrician. She pulled her cell phone out of the bag she'd brought outside with her and dialed his number.

The doctor told her if Missy wasn't any better in an hour, to bring her to his office.

"We're going in, Diane. But it was fun visiting with you."

"Yes, it was."

"Girls?" Jennifer called to the other two. "I want you to come in, too."

When they got inside, Jennifer raised the air conditioning and rubbed Missy's face with a cool, damp cloth. Steffi brought her sister a glass of water and Jennifer got her to drink some of it.

In a few minutes Missy cooled down some. Jennifer lay back on the sofa with her to watch television.

"Look, Mommy, there's a red light blinking," Steffi said, pointing to the answering machine.

"Go push it, Steffi," Jennifer said, her attention on Missy.

Nick's voice filled the room and a cheer went up from the three girls when they heard his invitation.

Chapter Eleven

The mere sound of his voice sent her heart racing in a rapid tattoo. Her mind furiously tried to calculate how many hours it would be till she saw him, but she could barely concentrate.

Nick was coming home!

The girls' excited voices brought her back to reality.

"I know you're excited about Nick's invitation, but I don't know if we can go. After all, Missy isn't feeling well."

"I feel much better, Mommy, I promise. *Please* let us go to dinner with Nick!"

"I can't promise you, Missy. I'll take your temperature later and if you don't have any fever, I'll consider it," she said firmly.

"But if Missy is okay, we can go?" Steffi asked.

Jennifer doubted the wisdom of accepting Nick's invitation, but she couldn't say no to the girls, not when she was fighting excitement herself. "Maybe."

Steffi leaned forward and said, "You'd better stay still and drink lots of water, Missy."

"I will," the child replied, already settling herself on the sofa. Her quiet didn't last long. In a few seconds she popped up and asked, "Will we go back to Chuck E. Cheese's?"

Jennifer shuddered. "I hope not. I think we should save that place for birthdays."

"When is your birthday, Mommy?" Missy asked.

"Later in the summer."

"What day is it?" Steffi needed more concrete information.

"It's August 2, honey. See, that's much later."

"What do you want for your birthday?" Annie asked. "I don't think you want a dolly like I did."

Jennifer smiled. "I don't want anything. I already have everything I'll ever need." She pulled the trio in for a quick, tight hug.

"What about a daddy?"

She leaned back and looked at Missy. "What do you mean?"

"Don't you want a daddy for your birthday?" Her brown eyes widened and twinkled. "I know just the daddy for you, too. Nick!"

Jennifer gasped and flushed like a lovesick teenager. "No!" When she noticed the offended look on Missy's face, she tempered her reply. "Thanks anyway, sweetheart. Why don't you just pick me some flowers instead?"

Missy seemed unconvinced. "But—"

"You need to rest if you want to go tonight. How about I put on a movie for you to watch."

"What movie?" Steffi asked.

"I think *Mary Poppins* would be a good movie to watch. It's about two children who need a nanny."

"What's a nanny?" Missy asked.

"It's a lady who takes care of children when their parents are too busy to take care of them."

Annie frowned. "Why would they be too busy?"

"You'll see when you watch the movie."

She went to the hall closet and got the DVD out and started it. The music reminded her of watching the movie when she was a little girl, wishing Mary Poppins had come to her house to weave her magic spell.

Once the movie got started, Jennifer tiptoed out of the room, leaving all three girls staring at the television screen.

With the music playing in the background, she kept busy, trying not to think of Nick returning.

As if she weren't counting the hours…

NICK LEANED FORWARD IN the back of the taxi, urging the vehicle closer and closer to home. That thought gave him pause. He'd only lived in the Dallas fourplex a couple of weeks. But it wasn't the place that was home. It was the people.

He wanted to see the girls, of course. But he especially wanted to see Jennifer. He wanted to throw his arms around her and give her a kiss that would let her know how much he'd missed her.

Only she seemed to be disturbed by his kisses. She'd let him get close for a minute, and then she'd pulled away the last time he'd kissed her.

He frowned. Something was bothering Jen. He wasn't sure what, but if he ever got some time to talk to her without six little ears listening in, he might have a chance to figure it out.

When the taxi finally pulled into the driveway, he paid the driver and grabbed his bag to hurry in to his apartment. He unlocked the door and threw his bag inside. Then he closed it and went to knock on Jennifer's door.

He heard little feet rushing toward the door, followed by Jennifer's voice warning them not to open it. He waited impatiently for Jennifer to look through the peephole.

He heard her unlocking the door and stepped forward as she swung it back. Before she could say anything, he pulled her into his embrace and kissed her.

"N-Nick, I didn't expect you back so soon!" Jennifer said as she pulled herself out of his arms.

Annie and Steffi ran to him, throwing themselves around his legs.

"Hi, girls," Nick said on a smile. "How've you been?"

"We're fine," Annie volunteered, "but Missy is sick."

"But we think she's well enough to go to dinner," Steffi hurriedly added.

Nick went at once to the sofa. "What's the matter, Missy?"

"Mommy says I'm sick, but I feel fine."

Jennifer came up to Missy from behind the sofa, keeping it between her and Nick. She leaned down to feel Missy's forehead. "I think she got overheated, but I have to be sure. Let me take your temperature, sweetie. If you're not running a fever, you can go out."

She went to get the thermometer. Once she left the room, Nick asked the girls how they'd managed while he was gone.

"We missed you," Missy told him.

"I missed all of you, too. It seemed like I was gone forever."

"I think Mommy missed you, too," Annie said quietly. "She doesn't smile as much when you're not here."

It was ridiculous to get one's hopes up based on a five-year-old's opinion, but he was desperate for any encouragement he could get.

When Jennifer came back into the room with a thermometer, he waited for her to take Missy's temperature.

"There's no fever," Jennifer announced, and the three little girls cheered.

"That means we can go!" Missy exclaimed.

"Terrific. Where do you want to go?"

The girls all looked at one another. "We don't want to go to Chuck E. Cheese's," Steffi said carefully.

"Ah, your mother already vetoed that one, did she?" he teased Jennifer, shooting her a grin. "That's good, because I was thinking about steak. Have you been to Outback?"

"What's that?" Missy asked.

"It's a steak place. The Outback is what they call the rural parts of Australia."

"What's Australia?" Steffi asked.

Jennifer stepped in. "That's a country a long way away. But they have good steaks there."

"In Australia?" Annie asked.

"No, here in Dallas at the restaurant, The Outback." Nick exchanged a smile with Jennifer. "Is that okay with you girls?"

"If Mommy likes it," Annie said.

Nick smiled at Jennifer. "Well, Mommy, what do you think?"

"It sounds lovely, but it's a little early for dinner. Shall we go in a couple of hours?"

"I guess I can wait that long." Nick wasn't sure. He didn't want to go back to his lonely apartment.

Annie seemed to understand. "You can play cards with us. Mommy got a new game."

"Sweetie, I don't think—" Jennifer began.

But Nick wasn't passing up an opportunity to stay. "I'd love to play cards with you, Annie."

"Me and Steffi get to play, too!" Missy insisted.

"Of course. And your mommy, too, if she wants to." Nick let his gaze move to Jennifer, hoping to see cooperation.

"I—I have some things to do. But you're welcome to play with the girls." She hurriedly left the room.

Nick stared after her until Missy tugged on his arm. "What, Missy?"

"Can you—" She looked at her older sister. "What does he have to do, Steffi?"

"Shuffle," she said.

"Oh, yeah, I can do that. Here," he said, holding out his hand for the deck of cards. "What game are we playing?"

"Go Fish!" Missy said with a giggle. "But we don't really hold fishes. That would by yucky!"

Nick grinned. He'd rather be spending time with Jennifer, he'd admit, but the girls were always fun. "Yes, it would, wouldn't it? And Mommy wouldn't like it because it would make a mess."

Steffi shook her head. "Mommy isn't fussy. My last mommy didn't even want us to sit on the furniture. She didn't seem to like anything we did. But Mommy just helps us clean up the messes and gives us kisses."

Nick sighed as he shuffled the cards. "Yeah, she's a really good mommy."

"Why didn't she already have kids?" Steffi asked.

As Nick considered his answer, Missy piped up. "'Cause she didn't have a daddy…until Daddy came." She pointed at Nick. "Are you going to have a baby?"

Nick felt heat rising up his neck. Just thinking about making a child with Jennifer raised his temperature.

"Are you, Daddy?" Missy prodded him.

"Uh, no, I mean, I'd like— I'm not married to Jennifer. That means no babies. Unless we get married," he couldn't help but add. He hadn't noticed Jennifer coming into the room as he made his last statement.

"What is going on in here?" Jennifer demanded.

Missy immediately thought she could explain, which sent fear through Nick's veins.

"We were talking about you and Daddy—I mean, Nick—having a baby because you're such a good mommy."

"It was Missy's idea, Mommy, not Nick's," Annie said, demonstrating her understanding of the situation. Maybe she was alerted by both the adults' red faces.

"I think I have enough to learn with you three, Missy. After I practice awhile we'll think about another child."

"But you have to have a daddy," Missy said, covertly looking at Nick.

"I didn't need one to get you, did I?"

"No, but—" Missy began until Nick caught her hand.

"Missy, I think your mommy is right. She needs some time to figure everything out. You're lucky she picked the three of you so you can be together." Nick smiled at the little girl so she'd know he wasn't chastising her.

Annie, in a soft voice, said, "Forever and ever."

"Yeah," Steffi agreed.

Jennifer smiled weakly at the girls. "Now I think you need to get that game started. I'd hate to miss my steak because the game hasn't ended."

Nick dealt the cards and hurried the game along. He was hungry, too.

For Jennifer.

WHEN THEY REACHED THE restaurant, Nick asked for a big booth.

"Are you sure, Nick?"

"It will be perfect. We'll put the girls on one side and you and me on the other."

"But I'll need to assist the girls."

"You can. The table isn't that wide." He was determined to have her beside him. He needed to at least get that close to her.

Jennifer helped each of her girls choose from the children's menu, and when they'd all placed their orders Nick asked the girls about their ballet and swimming lessons.

"Missy is the best swimmer," Jennifer said. "She's like a little fish. Steffi is the best at ballet. And we've started an art class and that's where Annie shines."

"Terrific. Something for everyone," Nick said with a smile. "And your mommy takes the best pictures."

"That reminds me," Jen said, "I'll pick up your photos tomorrow morning while the girls are in ballet class, if that's all right."

"That's fine. How did the housekeeper work out?"

"Oh, she's wonderful. She's coming to your apartment on Friday. Since you weren't here, you got last choice."

"That's fine. It means she can do my laundry from my trip."

"Did you have fun on your trip?" Missy asked.

"Not exactly, honey. I didn't go to California for fun. I had to work."

Jennifer turned to him with a look of disbelief. "All work and no play, Nick? In Hollywood?"

"They took me out for what they thought was fun, but I thought it was a waste of time. I wanted to get my work down and come home."

Jennifer put her head down, pretending to study her drink.

What was wrong with her? he wondered.

"What kind of work did you do?" Steffi asked.

"I was writing."

Missy nodded. "Writing is hard."

"Not for Nick, Missy. He's an adult," Steffi explained.

"Did you get the problem worked out?" Jennifer asked in a small voice.

"Yeah. It wasn't too hard."

"And they didn't offer you a job?" She finally looked at him.

He smiled at her. "Honey, my job is writing books, not screenplays."

"You can't do both?"

"Some people can, but I can't. It would be like you making portraits of people and taking aerial photos. Two different things."

"But you could train yourself to write screenplays, couldn't you?" Jennifer persisted.

"Maybe, but why would I want to?"

"So you could live in Hollywood," Jennifer said, as if he couldn't figure it out.

"I don't want to live in Hollywood."

"Why not?" she challenged him.

He turned the tables on her. "Would *you* want to live in Hollywood?"

"No, of course not. It would be a terrible place to raise children."

"I agree."

If they agreed, he wondered, why did Jen look so perturbed?

WHEN THEY GOT HOME, it was bedtime and Jennifer sent the children off to brush their teeth and put on their nightgowns.

Then she turned to Nick. "Thank you for a lovely evening." She almost put her hand out for him to shake, but she didn't think he'd buy that behavior. So she kept her hands around her purse in front of her.

"It was great, wasn't it? And I think the girls really liked it, too."

"Yes, of course. Well, I know you're anxious to settle back in your apartment, so I won't keep you." That was as obvious as she could be.

"No, I'm in no hurry. Can't I stay to help tuck the girls into bed?"

"Um, I—I suppose so."

They stood there awkwardly until they heard the girls call out, "We're ready."

Jennifer put her purse down on the sofa and went into the bedroom to kiss them good-night, followed by Nick.

By the time they left the bedroom, all the girls were smiling except for Jennifer.

She walked Nick back to the living room and tried her goodbye speech again.

"That's not going to work, Jennifer. We need to talk."

"About what?"

"I'm not sure, but something is bothering you."

Jennifer took a step away from Nick. "I don't know what you're talking about."

"You don't? Why are you moving away from me?"

She stood rooted in place, looking away from him. "I don't know what you mean."

"Yes, you do, and I'm not leaving until I get some answers."

"This is my apartment, Nick Barry. You can't threaten me in my own apartment!"

"I'm not threatening you, sweetheart. I just want some answers." He moved closer. "Can't we sit down and chat a few minutes?"

"It's late and—"

"Jennifer, it's eight-thirty!"

"Oh! I forgot because the girls go to bed early. I—I do, too, so I can get up early with them."

"I don't believe you."

She stared at him before dropping her glance. "Okay, we can talk for a few minutes."

She tried to reach the single chair in order to avoid sitting on the sofa with him, but he intercepted her. "Let's both sit here," he suggested.

"Fine!" she snapped, sitting down, her back straight and stiff.

He leaned near her. "Did you miss me while I was gone?"

"No, not at all."

"Jen, what's the point of talking if you're just going to lie to me?"

"I didn't—" She broke off as her gaze met his and she jerked it away. But she couldn't lie to him if she was meeting his gaze. "I didn't lie," she said, looking at her hands.

"Look me in my eyes and say that," he challenged.

"The—the girls missed you."

"I'm glad, but I didn't ask about the girls."

She tried to turn away, but he scooted closer and lifted a finger to pull her face around to his. "Didn't you miss me just a little bit?"

"Okay, fine, I missed you a little bit! Now—"

"Good," he said, just before he kissed her.

Somehow, before she knew it, her arms ended up around his neck and she was kissing him back. When he pulled her tighter to him, she didn't resist. Her mouth was open to his and she knew there was a reason to resist, but she couldn't quite remember what it was.

He pulled her onto his lap and wrapped his arms tightly around her as he reslanted his lips over hers to kiss her deeper than before. His hands wandered over her body, stroking her and encouraging her closer.

She felt as if she had melted onto him, as soft and

pliant as warm wax. If she pulled back, his imprint would be on her forever. But she wasn't pulling back. Instead, she was pressing against him, eager for more.

When his hand slipped below the short-sleeved sweater she'd worn to dinner, she almost convinced herself to protest, but his mouth moved more compellingly over hers, and she couldn't seem to bring herself to pull away.

"Jen, I missed you so much," he muttered as his lips moved to kiss her neck. Without his mouth on hers, she thought she could break the spell he had cast on her, but as she opened her mouth to do so, his lips returned to hers. She welcomed him like a long-lost lover.

Then, still kissing her, he stood and scooped her up in his arms.

"What are you doing?" she demanded in a whisper.

"I thought we'd be more comfortable in your bedroom," he murmured, still nibbling at her neck.

"No!" she said insistently, finally coming to her senses. "W-we can't do that. The girls might hear us! I can't—I shouldn't— Put me down!" While she kept her voice soft so she wouldn't disturb the girls, she was definite in her protest.

Nick let her slide down his body, still kissing her. She managed to pull away. But she was panting as if she'd just run a mile.

"Please—just go. I can't—"

"Okay," he agreed. "I guess we can stop here. But, Jennifer, you can't let the girls rule every aspect of your life. You have to have some personal time, too."

"Just go home, Nick," she said, trying to ignore the desperate plea in her words.

He kissed her again before he did as she asked. "Okay, I'll go home tonight. But we still need to have that talk. Something's bothering you, and I won't rest until I find out what it is."

A devastated Jennifer slumped against the closed door after Nick had left. She'd wanted to protect the girls from broken hearts, but she'd forgotten to protect her own. And she could definitely feel it cracking. No matter how much she wanted to, she couldn't believe Nick's words. Deep inside she believed Hollywood would prove to have too much allure and Nick would leave them behind.

Chapter Twelve

Nick had trouble settling down to his writing the next morning. Perhaps because he hadn't gone to sleep at his normal hour. He'd spent a lot of time thinking about Jennifer. He should've expected her to reject his intention to make love to her, but he hadn't. Somehow, he'd hoped she was feeling the same as him.

But not only was she not willing, she still hadn't told him why. Of course, it could be because he'd rushed her. He'd called himself all kinds of names as he'd realized that. But it hadn't made going to sleep any easier. His body was still on fire for hers.

After more than an hour, he managed to turn his thoughts to his book. He reread all that he'd written, which was five chapters. That took an hour. Then he was ready to write.

Only there was a knock on his door.

When he answered it, he found Jennifer standing on his doorstep. He swung the door wide.

"Come in."

She stood her ground. "I just wanted to give you the copies of your photos you wanted."

He refused to take the package she held out. "I have to pay you first. How much was the paper and film?"

"I think we agreed on twenty-five dollars, but you can pay me later," she hurriedly said.

"No, come in. I just need to find my checkbook."

She reluctantly entered his apartment.

"Are the girls napping?" he asked.

"No, but the housekeeper is with them," Jennifer said. Then she suddenly got an edgy look on her face.

"I'm not going to attack you, Jen, so stop looking so apprehensive. Of course, I wouldn't resist a kiss or two."

"No, that's okay," Jennifer took a quick step backward.

He grinned and came closer, unable to resist temptation. "Just one kiss? That wouldn't be too bad, would it?"

"You never stop at one kiss," she pointed out.

"I promise I will this morning unless you say differently."

"I don't think that's a good idea."

"I do." And he bent his head to kiss her. As he did so, his arms went around her, pulling her tight against him.

She was determined to protest after the first kiss, but she was the one who forgot. It wasn't until he lifted his lips from hers that she realized he was honoring his promise.

"I— Thank you."

He grinned. "You don't have to thank me, honey. I'm willing to kiss you anytime."

"I was thanking you for stopping after one kiss, not for the kiss." Her cheeks turned bright red.

"Are you willing to tell me why you don't want me to kiss you?"

"I don't think that's appropriate behavior for a mother," she said, backing away again.

"I think it is. After all, she had to do a lot of kissing to get the children in the first place."

"For most mothers, but not for me!"

"Which means you need to practice even more," he said with a grin.

"No! No, it doesn't. They won't ever know that."

"So if you grow old alone, they won't blame themselves for causing you to sacrifice your happiness for them?"

"Of course not! You're being ridiculous!"

"I don't think so. Annie said you didn't smile as much while I was gone. They notice these things."

"Annie said that? You're not making it up?"

"I swear she did."

"Well, it's not true."

"So you hate my guts and like it when I'm not around?"

"No, of course not."

She was looking very uncomfortable.

"So you like for me to kiss you?"

"Nick, I need to go. I'll get your check later." And she left his apartment.

He stood there, his hands in his pockets, staring at the door. He couldn't help teasing her, but he believed there was some attraction there. He could feel it when he held her close. But there was something keeping them apart.

He'd just have to figure it out.

THE SECOND NICK PICKED UP the ringing phone, his agent cut right to business.

"How was Hollywood?" Jim asked.

"Fine."

"An all-expenses-paid trip to Hollywood and all you can say is 'Fine'? And you call yourself a writer!"

Nick laughed in spite of himself. "It was good, but I was in a hurry to get home."

"You've only lived in Dallas for a few weeks. What could— Ah, a woman."

Nick grinned. "Yeah. So?"

"A new acquaintance?"

"I met her the first day I moved in."

Jim's voice sobered. "Just remember what I told you. You've worked hard for your money. You don't want some gold digger after you."

"Not to worry." Jennifer didn't want his money. In fact she didn't want anything from him.

"The guys in Hollywood are interested in you staying awhile longer the next time you're out there," Jim said.

"I'm not planning on going back anytime soon."

"They called me this morning to hint that they could use you out there until they finish filming."

"No, thanks."

"Nick, if the woman's that important to you, you can take her with you. I wouldn't think she'd turn down a trip to Hollywood."

"This woman would. Besides, they have tons of writers in Hollywood. They don't need me to turn my book into a screenplay."

"Aren't you worried about how the film will turn out?"

"Aren't you the agent who told me to look upon money from Hollywood as a blessing, but not to get too caught up in them doing a faithful translation from book to screen?"

"Okay, I just thought I should ask. How's the new book going?"

"I just got back last night. It'll take a while to get moving on it again, but I don't think my deadline is in jeopardy."

"Okay. Let me know if you run into problems."

"Will do."

Nick hung up the phone and sat staring at the wall. No, Jennifer wasn't the kind to pick up and fly to Hollywood. Not with the three little girls in tow. He agreed with her that Hollywood was not the place for children. It was flattering that they were interested in him, but he had no intention of moving to Hollywood.

The more interesting stories were to be found right here.

BILLS, CREDIT CARD applications, advertisements.

All the usual suspects in the mail today, she thought as she thumbed through the stack…till she came to a small manila envelope with a familiar scrawl. She recognized the handwriting; it was her uncle's.

Could it be…?

She'd just about given up that her uncle, or social services, would scare up the photo of the girls' parents that Steffi wanted so badly. With each passing day she'd held out less and less hope that she'd be able to come through on her promise to Steffi.

Her hand was shaking when she opened the clasp on the envelope and pulled out a handwritten note: "Did the best I could. Sorry it took so long." It was signed by her uncle, and paper-clipped to a long thin strip of cheap photo paper. Jennifer looked at the photos, the kind taken in one of those booths at a carnival or boardwalk. Three different poses of a young couple, yet unmistakably Steffi, Annie and Missy's parents, judging by the uncanny resemblance of the girls to the woman in the photo.

She couldn't tell where or when the pictures had been taken, but she could see how happy the couple was, how much in love. Tears filled her eyes and spilled down her cheeks, and she let them come. She let herself cry for their loss, for the years that were taken away, for the children they'd never get to see grow up.

I'll look after them, she silently promised the smiling

couple. I'll always make sure they're safe and they never forget you.

She'd have to find the perfect moment to give the photo to Steffi.

And to thank her uncle for the miracle he worked in getting it.

She took out stationery and began writing a note to him, all the while counting her blessings for having someone in her family who was on her side. Too bad her mother couldn't be. But at least she had decent odds—fifty percent of her family supported her.

What about your half brother? asked an inner voice. What would he think?

She remembered then something Nick had said recently, how she shouldn't let fear of rejection stop her from contacting her half brother. Her father had been wrong in denying a meeting between them, Nick had said.

For a while now she couldn't get thoughts of William Carpenter out of her head.

Maybe this was a sign, she thought as she gazed down at her uncle's note. He'd come through for her and given her something so precious. Perhaps she ought to reach out to a new member of her family. After all, hadn't she always vowed not to be like either of her parents? By distancing herself from her half brother she was following her dad's behavior. If she thought he was wrong, why was she acting like him?

That bothered her. And there was also the fact that

if Nick was going to go away as she thought he would, it might be good for the girls to know another man. Annie especially needed to know that men, other than Nick, wouldn't hurt her.

Today, she'd decided, she'd reach out to her brother.

William had been eleven when her father had died, eight years ago. Jennifer had been nineteen, the age her half brother was now. A lot of years had passed, a lot of growing up, reflecting. The only way to know how her half brother felt now was to bite the bullet and call. And there was no time like the present. She put down the pen and dialed the number for her father's widow.

When she answered, Jennifer took a deep breath and identified herself. Then she asked to speak to William.

"He's in class right now, Jennifer. Is there something I can help you with?"

The woman sounded pleasant, unlike her own mother whenever Jennifer had mentioned her ex-husband's wife.

"I—I just wanted to contact him," she said, trying hard to keep up her courage. "I thought he might be interested in getting to know me."

After a moment the woman asked, "Does your mother know you're calling him?"

"I don't live with my mother and she has nothing to do with me."

"I see. Well, I'll ask him to call you. I can't be sure he will."

Jennifer gave her her telephone number and her

address. "I'd like to meet him. I promise I won't do anything to hurt him."

"I'll give him your message," was all the woman said.

Jennifer was shaking when she hung up the phone. She had to remind herself to breathe as she stood up and went to get a glass of water. No one knew how William would react to the message, even if her father's widow would relay it. But Jennifer had done her part. She'd taken the first step. Now only time would tell.

As she turned to put the glass in the sink, she saw Steffi come into the room.

"You got up early, sweetheart. And you seemed so tired after your ballet lesson today." Her eyes shot to the envelope and photo on the table, and Steffi's followed.

"If you're busy, I can go back to my room," she said, ever the adult child.

Jennifer deliberated. She could buy herself some time and plan how she would give the photo to Steffi, or she could just let her heart be her guide. As she looked at the girl, she opted for the latter.

"No, Steffi, I'm not busy. I'm never too busy for you." She held out her hand and when Steffi took it, she led them to the sofa in the living room. Along the way she pocketed the photo strip.

"What is it, Jennifer? Is everything okay?" Steffi looked at her with deep brown eyes that seemed to see more than a six-year-old should.

Jennifer smiled. "Everything is fine. Wonderful, in fact." She reached into her pocket and fingered the photo. "Steffi, you remember when I told you I'd do my best to find a picture of your parents? Well, I…I did it, honey." She took the photo out and proffered it. "Will this one do?"

Slowly Steffi reached for the precious gift. For a few moments she said nothing, merely looked at it, and Jennifer's throat tightened. Had she done the wrong thing? Was it too much for the girl? Would the photo bring back memories of untold sadness, grief? She reached out for Steffi, her hand shaking.

"Steffi, are you okay?"

The little girl looked up at her, and a small smile split her face. "I look just like her. Look, Jennifer. Do you see?"

Jennifer let out a breath she didn't know she was holding. "I see, baby," she said through a smile.

"And there are three pictures. One for each of us. Wait till I show Annie and Missy."

What an amazing child, Jennifer thought. And what an amazing set of parents to have raised such wonderful, thoughtful children. She wrapped her arms around the girl. "Why don't you go show them, Steffi?"

The girl got up from the sofa, but before she ran down the hall she looked at Jennifer. "Thank you," she said simply.

It was all Jennifer needed to hear.

THE APARTMENT SMELLED AS good as a bakery. Zucchini bread was cooling on the counter, the cookie jar was filled and Jennifer was icing a cake. It was what she did whenever she got restless: she baked. And the girls loved it. They'd already had more than their weekly allotment of cookies. She drew a deep breath and stood just as Annie came into the living room.

She stepped back to admire her handiwork when the doorbell rang.

"I'll get it," she called to the girls, hoping to stop the wild rush to the door that was typical of them.

The three girls remained in front of the television, the cookies and lemonade holding them in place.

She swung the door open, expecting to see Nick. Instead, she stared at a stranger.

A familiar stranger. "Yes?"

"Are you Jennifer?"

"Yes, I am."

"I'm William, but most everyone calls me Billy." He held out a hand to her.

She couldn't stop the tears from flowing. All afternoon she'd been afraid to hope, afraid that he wouldn't call her back, afraid that he would. What would they say to each other? How would they act?

But here he was in front of her, a smile on his face, his hand outstretched as if to bridge the years they'd been apart.

She took it in her own. "I'm so happy to see you," she gushed, wiping her tears. "Won't you come in?" She opened the door wide and ushered him into the apartment.

"Something smells good in here," he remarked, looking around.

"I've been baking." An understatement, but he didn't need to know how nervous she'd been. "If you go outside on the deck, I'll bring out some cookies and lemonade and we can talk." She smiled at him. "Get to know each other."

"Sounds good." He followed the path she pointed out.

As Jennifer got a tray prepared, she told Mrs. Carroll where she would be. After that, she explained to the girls that she was going outside to visit with her guest.

When she reached the deck, she set the tray down on the table. "I appreciate your visiting me, Billy. I— I had asked my dad once for us to be family, but he didn't think it would be a good idea."

"Why?" Billy asked with a frown.

"I think it was because of my mother. She's…rather difficult."

"Oh, yeah, my mom said."

Jennifer smiled. "I know. But I thought it might help you, as well as me, to know each other. We probably have some things in common because of our dad."

"Yes, I think so, too." He looked down and swirled the ice in his glass. "Dad never mentioned you to me. I never knew who you were, not even at the funeral."

Jennifer tried to hide her hurt.

"But my mom knew about you," Billy hurriedly said. "She said you were beautiful, and she was right."

"Thank you, Billy. I actually think we look quite alike except for my blond hair. Yours is brown, like Dad's."

"Yeah, we do. Did you get your blond hair from your mom?"

"Yes."

"Does she live here, too?"

"No, this is where your grandmother lived. I don't think Dad ever introduced you to her because she disapproved of his divorce."

"Is she alive now?"

"No, I'm sorry. She died about two years ago."

"I wish I'd met her."

"Yes, she would've liked that, too. But she believed you only got married once and if you were miserable, too bad."

"Ah, old-fashioned."

"Yes, she was, but she was a dear."

They chatted for a half hour, and Jennifer was glad to discover that her father had left his second wife and son well-provided for. Billy was attending Southern Methodist University, here in Dallas, and driving a Porsche.

They were laughing over something their father had done when the door to the deck slammed back against the wall, surprising them.

Nick stomped out on the deck.

"Why, Nick, is something wrong?" Jennifer asked.

"I heard you were entertaining. I thought maybe your mother had invited someone to meet you."

It took her a minute to figure out what he meant, but

then she laughed. "No. Actually, this is your fault. You encouraged me to contact my half brother. Billy, this is Nick Barry, my neighbor."

Billy stood and offered his hand.

Nick stared at him. "Your brother?"

"Yes, Nick, my brother."

Nick shook his hand. "I'm delighted to meet you," he said, his gaze shifting back to Jennifer.

Jennifer actually giggled.

Billy said, "I don't understand why you're laughing."

"Oh, I'm sorry. My mother has been trying to set me up with a man, and apparently Nick thought it was you."

Billy's gaze shifted to Nick. "No, you're still in luck," he said with a smile.

They stood there for a moment, then Billy said, "Aren't you going to ask Nick to join us?"

"Thanks, Billy. Don't mind if I do." Nick sat down before reaching out to take a cookie. "Hey, these are good. Did you make them, Jen?"

"Yes, I did. I guess now I have to go get you some lemonade. I'll be right back."

"Do you think she sounded irritated?" Nick asked Billy.

The boy smiled. "Not much. And I don't blame you for charging to the rescue. Any man her mother would choose, according to my mother, would be terrible."

"You've met her mother?"

"No, have you?"

"Yeah, accidentally. We were coming back from a

shopping trip with the girls and her mother cornered her in the parking lot."

"The girls?"

"You didn't meet her three little girls?" Nick asked in surprise.

"She has children? I didn't know she'd been married before."

"She hasn't." Nick raised a hand at Billy's astonishment. "I'd better tell you before she gets out here and you think she's a scarlet woman. She's adopting three little sisters. They're adorable."

Just then the door opened and Jennifer brought a glass of lemonade for Nick and more cookies.

"Oh, good. I was hungry but I didn't think I should take the last one," Nick said.

"Yes, I was relying on your excellent manners. Now you don't have to hold back," she said.

Both males grinned at her and reached for more cookies.

"Of course, you're going to ruin your dinner if you eat too many."

Nick winked at Billy. "She only has girls. If she had boys, she'd know better."

"And I don't have to worry about dinner because Mom's going out tonight and I'm all on my own," Billy said.

"I'm all on my own, too," Nick said mournfully.

"Stop it, Nick! You're always on your own."

"Oh, yeah, I forgot."

"Billy, you're welcome to have dinner with us. I want to introduce you to my three girls."

"Yeah, Nick explained. I'd love to meet them."

"Does that mean I'm *not* invited to dinner?" Nick asked.

Jennifer sent him a disgusted look. "I shouldn't reward such a ridiculous ploy for an invitation, but yes, you are invited to dinner, too, Nick."

"Terrific! I bet the girls are having cookies right now, too."

Jennifer's cheeks flamed. "Yes, they had ballet lessons this morning to use up their energy."

"She's a great mother, Billy, and she had no experience at all," Nick assured him.

"I bet she is. But, Jennifer, how did you come to adopt three little girls?"

She explained about The Heart Gallery photos and how she'd discovered Annie was being abused.

Billy looked terribly upset, but then she told him how well they'd done in the past few weeks, and how Nick had helped Annie overcome her fear of men.

"I can't wait to meet them. They sound wonderful."

"You'll be their uncle," Jennifer said. "They've never had one of those."

"Wait, that makes Billy more important than me," Nick mock-protested.

"Nick, it's not a contest."

"That's true, besides I'm their daddy." He gave her a sly grin.

"No, you aren't and you shouldn't say that. It'll give Billy the wrong idea."

Nick explained how Missy had met him in the hall.

"That must've been a shock to you," Billy said.

"Yes, it was. But then I met your sister, which was a wonderful thing."

"Listen, gentlemen, if I'm going to get dinner done in time, I have to start cooking."

"Why don't I take Billy to my apartment, so he'll be out of your way? We can visit on our own."

She looked at Nick suspiciously. "Are you up to something?"

"Not me. Just offering to help."

"Okay. But, Billy, if you don't want to talk to Nick, just come back across the hall."

He grinned. "I think I'll be safe."

She took the tray, with the three glasses on it, back inside. Over her shoulder at the two men following her, she tossed, "Be back at six for dinner."

"We will. If I don't scare him away before then." Nick wiggled his brows when Jennifer turned around. Then he led Billy over to his place. "Are you working or going to school, Billy?"

"I go to SMU."

"Nice school." Nick pointed to the leather sofa. "Have a seat. Are you old enough to drink coffee?"

"Sure, how else would I stay awake before exams?" Billy asked, grinning at Nick.

"I understand completely. I'll put on a pot."

When he returned a few minutes later, he carried two mugs of coffee. "I didn't bring any cookies because I don't bake like Jen does. Besides, I don't want to be accused of ruining your appetite."

Billy accepted a cup of coffee. Then he looked at Nick. "So, you're in love with Jennifer?"

Chapter Thirteen

Nick sat down on the sofa and stared at Billy. "How'd you know?"

Billy grinned. "Trust me. It's pretty obvious."

"Is it a problem?"

"I don't know. Can you support her and three kids?"

"Yeah."

"What do you do?"

Nick cleared his throat. It was time to tell the truth. "Uh, I'm a writer." He gave Billy all the details of the film deal. Then he asked, "Is there anything else you want to ask me?"

"Hey, I'm kind of new at this brother thing. What else *should* I ask?"

"How about do I want children?" Nick suggested.

"Isn't that a given since she already has three?"

"Oh, yeah."

"Well?"

Nick shrugged his shoulders. "I can't think of anything else for you to ask. Do you have a girlfriend?"

"Hey, you're turning the tables on me!"

"I've never had a brother, so I have to practice, too."

"So you're an only child, too?"

Nick shook his head. "No, I have three sisters."

"How old are they?"

"Twenty-six."

"And?"

"And what?"

"Well, you said you had three sisters but you only gave me one age."

"They're triplets," Nick said with a grin.

"Wow! I've never known triplets!"

"They're too old for you, junior," Nick teased.

Billy laughed. "You're right. Besides, I do have a girlfriend, but don't tell my mother."

"Ah. Something to blackmail you with."

BY THE TIME JENNIFER opened the door to the two men invited to dinner, they seemed to be quite happy with each other.

"So, you found something to talk about for two hours?" she asked, giving each of them a close look.

When Nick and Billy laughed and nodded, she decided not to ask their topic of conversation. Instead she ushered Billy into the living room.

"I want you to meet my three daughters, Steffi, Annie and Missy."

"Hi, girls. I'm Billy."

"Hi," Steffi said.

Annie was shy again, edging toward Nick, and Missy crossed her arms over her chest. "Mommy said you're our uncle. But we don't got no uncles. Well, I did have one, but I didn't like him."

"Missy, he's not like that uncle," Jennifer hurriedly said. Then she turned to Billy. "That was in her foster family."

"I see. Well, I'll try to be really nice, Missy. Okay?"

"Okay, but we like Nick better."

"Missy, this is not a competition. We can have Nick as a neighbor and Billy as your uncle." Jennifer rolled her eyes at Nick.

"It's not my fault!" Nick protested.

"I'm not sure I believe you," Jennifer said. "Come in and be seated. We're ready to eat."

"We're eating at the big table tonight," Missy pointed out.

"She means the dining room," Jennifer clarified.

"Ah. It's my first time for the dining room, too," Nick pointed out.

"So you've eaten with them before?" Billy asked him.

"A number of times, but we ate in the kitchen or we ate out."

"One time we went to Chuck E. Cheese's for my birthday," Annie said softly.

"That sounds like fun. I haven't been there in ages."

That won Missy over. She clapped her hands and grinned at her new uncle.

Jennifer just shook her head. "I thought we could eat a real meal tonight."

"I'll vote for it," Billy said. "What's for dinner, Jen?"

"Roast beef, whipped potatoes, macaroni and cheese and salad. It's a little heavy on the carbohydrates, but the girls like them."

"We do, too," Billy said with a grin.

Once they were seated at the table, the children on their best behavior, Jennifer told the girls that Billy went to college.

"What's that?" Missy asked.

"It's where you go after you go to high school," Nick explained.

"Did you go to college?" Steffi asked.

"Yes, I did. And your mommy did, too."

"You did, Mommy?"

"Yes, Steffi, and you will, too. It helps you get a good job when you're older."

"Billy hasn't chosen his major yet," Nick said.

"Oh, really? What are you leaning toward, Billy?" Jennifer asked.

"I think business. My strengths are in math and science."

"You could do a lot with those strengths," Jennifer said.

"Maybe. I'm just not sure."

"Maybe you could go to work for the FBI," Nick suggested.

"Nick! Why would you suggest such a thing?" Jennifer stared at him, horrified.

"I've read that they take people with all different majors."

"But that could be dangerous."

"I think it sounds like fun. I'll have to look into that," Billy said, his eyes lighting up.

"Your mother will never forgive me if you go to work for the FBI. Please tell her that it wasn't my idea."

Nick and Billy exchanged a look that irritated Jennifer. "What does that mean? That look!"

"It's because you're acting like a girl, Jen," Nick said.

"I am a girl!" Jennifer almost shouted. "I thought you'd noticed that!"

He grinned and his eyes seemed to twinkle. "Oh, I did. I definitely did."

"Nicholas Barry, you're asking for trouble."

"I just meant that Billy will only show more interest when you mention danger. That's not how to discourage him."

"I could tell him he'd be nothing more than a paper-pusher, but now he wouldn't believe me." Nick crunched a forkful of salad and looked at Billy. "Maybe you'd be better off with a job that puts you in contact with a lot of women."

"You think he wants to be a hairdresser?" Jennifer demanded.

Billy put up his hands. "Hey, that's not me!"

She grinned in return. "I didn't think so."

"That's okay. Make enough money and the women will find you," Nick assured him.

"Like Nick," Jennifer pointed out.

"Right. I was captured by a woman the first night I moved in, right, Missy?"

The girls hadn't been following the conversation since they really didn't understand it. When Missy heard Nick call her name, she looked up.

"Tell Billy how I met you, Missy."

"I found him! I thought he could be our new daddy."

"Sounds like a plan to me," Billy said with a smile and a wink to Nick.

Jennifer ignored both of them, opting to focus on the children. "Steffi, you need to eat some of your salad as well as macaroni and cheese."

"Yes, Mommy," Steffi said. .

Annie piped up as she saw Jennifer look her way. "I ate my salad."

"Yes, you did, sweetie. That means you get dessert."

"I ate my salad," Nick pointed out. "Do I get dessert, too?"

"I was just kidding. Everyone does."

Jennifer got up and began taking dishes to the kitchen.

"I'll help while you entertain the girls," Nick told Billy. Then he took dishes to the kitchen, too.

"There's no need to help, Nick," Jennifer said when he put the plates in the sink. "I can do it."

"I wanted to. It gives me a chance to kiss you," he said, and immediately kissed her before she could protest. "I'll go get the rest of the dishes now." He left her standing there, speechless.

When he brought the rest of the dishes in, she made sure to keep her back to him. "Please take in that stack of cake plates and forks."

"Yes, ma'am," he agreed, apparently realizing she wasn't going to give him another chance to kiss her.

She followed him with a chocolate cake.

"Oh, goody!" Annie applauded when she saw the cake. "It's beautiful, Mommy. Is it someone's birthday?"

"Not a birthday," she replied, smiling warmly at Billy, "but it is a special occasion." An occasion she'd waited many long years for. In a sense, she realized she owed it to Nick. He'd given her the courage to make the call.

After dessert she ushered everyone into the living room while she loaded the dishwasher.

"Need some help?" Nick asked, sneaking up behind her.

She started. "I don't think I need your kind of help."

"I promise, I'm only in here to help with the dishes," he said, understanding her words at once.

"No, really, Nick, it's not necessary. Go talk to Billy or—" It dawned on her that maybe Nick had had enough of this little family reunion. "You can go home if you want."

"I don't. I want to stay here with you. I had a lot of time on my own in Hollywood."

"That's the last place I thought you'd be alone."

"Jen, contrary to what you're implying, there were no women around me in Hollywood."

"I've heard the women there are all blond and beautiful."

"I've seen more beautiful blondes here. In fact, I'm looking at one right now."

His eyes feasted on her, from head to toe. Every place they touched went on fire in their incendiary wake. Jennifer couldn't breathe in the suddenly too-hot kitchen.

He walked toward her and she was convinced he would take her in his arms again. Her lips parted for his.

Instead, he reached out for the dishes, taking them from her hands. "I'll do this. You go get to know your brother. You've waited a long time for this day."

He led her to the living room where she took a seat next to Billy on the sofa. The girls were watching TV, which gave them time to talk.

When the show ended, Jennifer had the girls tell their guests good-night. Nick collected a hug from each of them before they went to get ready for bed.

When they were alone, Billy said to him, "Looks like you're in around here."

Nick grinned. "I'm trying."

"You really don't mind taking on a ready-made family?"

He clapped the young man on the back. "Billy, my friend, I'm looking forward to it."

SHE'D COME CLOSE. Too close.

The incident in the kitchen had nearly been the Undoing of Jennifer Carpenter.

If Nick had reached out for her, she'd have been powerless to resist the allure of his arms, his lips.

It would've been the best kiss of her life.

And the biggest mistake.

She'd had to remind herself that night, and every night since, that what she needed from Nick Barry was distance.

After all, it would only be a matter of time before he followed the lure to Hollywood.

But when she checked her mail a couple of days later, she couldn't help sharing her excitement with him. She crossed the hall to knock on his door.

He opened it and greeted her with a smile. "Hi, what's up?"

"Look what I got in the mail."

He took the pale blue envelope and opened it. Inside was an invitation to The Heart Gallery showing of the portraits the various photographers in the Dallas area had made of the foster children.

"Is your picture of the girls going to be in it?"

"Yes! That's why I'm excited. It's like free advertising for me. My business cards will be beside the photo."

"That's terrific, honey. Will the girls go with you?"

"Yes, and I wondered if you wanted to go, too. It would help to have an extra pair of eyes on the girls."

"I'd love to go. When is it?"

"It's next Friday evening. Oh! The girls and I need to go shopping! I hadn't thought of that."

"Definitely a woman," he said with a smile.

"What?"

"That's always a woman's first thought—what will I wear?"

She frowned. "You keep making these sexist remarks."

"Not sexist, honey. It's all in admiration."

"I'm not sure I believe you."

"Do you need some help with the girls on the shopping trip? It sounds like fun to me."

"But you've got your writing to do. I can't—"

"I need a break. I've been writing a lot the past few days. I'd enjoy some time off."

"You're sure?"

"I'm sure. When do you want to go?"

"I think after lunch. They'll miss their naps, but that will be better than going after dinner. Do you want to come to lunch before we go?"

"I'd love to."

"You didn't even ask what we're having."

"Doesn't matter."

Half an hour later, they were all sitting around the table, eating.

"Why do we have to go shopping? I want to play with Blondie," Missy asked.

"Because we're going to see the pictures everyone

made of the foster children, and I want you to look nice. So we're buying you all new clothes."

"Oh. Will our picture be there?"

"Yes, Missy, it will."

"But we've already seen it."

"Yes, but I want to see the other pictures. It may give me some ideas."

Nick said nothing, letting Jennifer handle her children.

With a big sigh of suffering, Missy said, "Okay."

"Thank you, Missy. And we'll try to get home for you to play with Blondie after dinner."

When they reached the mall, Nick again let Jennifer take the lead, choosing the store she wanted to shop in. It was the same store where they'd bought the girls' shoes. He sat down in the chair just outside the dressing rooms and promised to wait for them to emerge. After a few minutes, Missy came out and crawled into his lap.

"I'm tired."

"You can take a nap as long as Mommy has already found you a dress."

"Yes, it's very pretty. It's blue with pink roses on it."

"It sounds lovely."

She lay her head on his shoulder, and Nick began to gently sway, rocking her to sleep.

When the other girls came out with Jennifer, dresses in hand, she continued on to pay for her purchases. The girls waited with Nick and Missy, who was still sleeping. Annie leaned against Nick and Steffi looked at things close by.

When Jennifer came back with her hands full, Nick told Steffi to hold Annie's hand and Annie should hold on to Jennifer's purse.

"Oh, good, I hadn't thought of that."

"It's a trick my mother used when her hands were full," he said with a grin.

"Do we need to wake Missy up?" Jennifer asked. "Is she too heavy?"

"No, she's fine. Did you find anything for yourself?"

"Oh, I have things to wear. I think a nice suit will look professional."

"Absolutely."

"Thanks, Nick. I know I'm taking advantage of you, but—"

"I wouldn't have it any other way."

"You're very generous with your time."

"I enjoy it. Now, how about we go by the ice cream shop and everyone gets something good, like maybe a malt?"

"What's a malt?" Steffi asked him.

"Oh, honey, it's the best." He looked to Jen. "What do you say, Mommy? It'll be my treat for such efficient shopping."

"You shouldn't— Oh, okay. The girls do deserve a treat."

"And so do you."

She giggled. "I never could resist a chocolate malt. It's my favorite flavor. What's yours?"

Her question was innocent enough, so was her expression, but Nick's mind took him on a sensuous direction. His favorite flavor? Her. He could still taste her on his lips. And he wanted more.

NICK DRESSED IN A SUIT before he knocked on Jennifer's door on Friday night.

When she opened the door, she raised her eyebrows. She really hadn't seen him all dressed up except when he put on the shirt and suit coat for his picture. "Oh, my. You look quite impressive," Jennifer said.

"Thank you, ma'am. I believe I can return that compliment, except you look better than impressive."

"Are you ready for the most impressive group?" she teased.

He nodded.

"Girls? Are you ready?"

Three little blond beauties appeared, their hair beautifully styled, their dresses highlighting their charms.

"Wow! You look great, girls. I'm a lucky guy to escort the four most beautiful girls ever."

"That's when we say thank you, girls," Jen told them, "even though his compliment was a little over the top." But the smile she gave him made it all worthwhile.

When they reached the hall where the photos were being shown, they found a crowd milling around, examining the portraits hung on the walls.

"Where's our picture?" Missy asked, impatient. She was ready to charge through the crowd. Annie hung back, clutching Nick's hand. Steffi walked beside Jennifer, watching everyone with awe.

"We'll find our picture in a moment," Jennifer said, looking at the first portraits on the wall. They were all beautifully done, each one influenced by the person behind the camera.

Nick knew he was prejudiced, but, having seen the portrait Jennifer had done of the three girls, he felt her work was better than anything he saw on the walls around him.

As they moved through the room, Nick began to notice the stares the girls were receiving. He guessed they were being recognized from their portrait. He couldn't hold back a smile. They were beautiful children, of course, but they had become more beautiful with Jennifer's love and care.

He was proud to be with them.

When they finally reached their portrait, there was a crowd around it, which made it impossible for the girls to see.

"But I can't see me!" Missy protested.

"Me, neither," Steffi said.

"Here, I'll lift you up one at a time," Nick said, starting with Missy. They were drawing attention, but he thought the girls should get to see their picture in such a public place. Then he set Missy down and picked up Annie. Before he could get to Steffi, the crowd had parted so the girls could see the picture.

A couple was whispering to each other, pointing out

the girls. Then the lady stepped forward. "These must be the three sisters pictured here."

"Yes, they are," Nick said. "And here's the photographer, Jennifer Carpenter."

The couple shook Jennifer's hand, congratulating her on her excellent work. Then the woman said, "My husband and I think the girls are so beautiful and precious." She beamed at Jennifer. "So we want to adopt them."

Chapter Fourteen

Like a mother bear protecting her cubs, Jennifer advanced on the woman. "You'll do no such thing!" she exclaimed.

Nick stepped forward, trying to defuse the volatile confrontation. "What Ms. Carpenter means is that the girls have already been taken."

"You mean someone has adopted them?" the woman asked.

"Well, they're going through the process."

"Who is it?"

Nick wasn't sure what to say, but Jennifer had no doubt. "*I* am the one adopting them."

"You and your husband?"

"No. I'm not married, but they assured me—"

"We're a married couple. I think we might be better prospects," the woman pointed out.

Nick reached for Jennifer. "Don't say anything else, Jen," he whispered.

Then he smiled at the woman, "If you'll excuse us, we want to see the other portraits." He led his little family away from the couple.

"I didn't like them," Missy said.

"Me, neither," Annie added.

Steffi said, "Let's go home."

"Why don't you three come with me and we'll go get another malt while Mommy looks at the other portraits."

The girls all readily agreed. Jennifer seemed torn. "I—I'm not sure I want to stay."

"Go ahead and look at the other portraits. We'll be back in half an hour and we'll bring you a chocolate malt." He hugged her for support, then with the girls all holding hands, he led them out of the gathering.

He felt sorry for Jennifer. She had so looked forward to the evening. She hadn't expected a challenge to her adoption of the girls.

"Is Mommy sad?" Annie asked.

"Why would you ask that, Annie?" Nick hedged.

"Because she seemed upset with that lady."

"Well, the lady thought she wanted to adopt all three of you."

Missy popped up from the backseat. "You mean that lady wants to take us away from Mommy?" she demanded, outrage in her voice.

"I don't think she can do it, Missy. Mommy has already applied to adopt you. I think she'll get to do so."

"I hope so," Steffi said.

"Me, too," Annie whispered.

"I know all of you love Mommy and want to be her children. I can assure you Mommy will do everything she can to keep you."

They went through the drive-through and got five malts, three child-size and two adult-size. Afterward, they drove back to the exhibit and parked in front so they could look for Jennifer when she came out.

It didn't take too long for Jennifer to emerge. Nick's heart ached for her. Gone was that excited air she'd worn into the exhibit. Now she looked sad, discouraged, worried. He wanted to wrap his arms around her and tell her everything would be all right. But he couldn't.

There was a chance that the woman was right. Maybe the courts would look more favorably on a married couple. But Jennifer had taken in the girls for all the right reasons. The woman in the gallery had voiced a selfish reason for adopting the girls. She and her husband apparently owned a clothing line and thought they'd get advertising mileage out of adopting the girls and using them as models.

Jennifer got in the car, and Nick handed her her chocolate malt.

"Thanks," she said, sitting quietly and sipping her drink.

By the time they got home, Annie was crying silently in the backseat, Steffi was sniffing and Missy was mad.

Nick picked up Annie to carry her in. Jennifer took the other two by their hands and headed into her apartment.

As always, Missy was the outspoken one. "But, Mommy, it's not fair. You said we don't need a daddy, right?"

"Missy, I don't know. I'm going to call on Monday and see what they say."

"Don't worry about it, Missy. Mommy will find a way to keep you, I promise," Nick said.

"Really?" Missy asked.

"Really." He looked at the other girls. "Everything's going to be all right," he said firmly.

Annie nodded and Steffi said, "I believe you, Nick."

"Good. Now, go get ready for bed so Mommy can tuck you in."

When the girls left the room, Jennifer looked at him. "I appreciate the effort, Nick, but you shouldn't have promised them."

"Why not?"

"Because what if the courts do favor a married couple over a single woman?"

"Don't you want to keep the girls?" he asked.

"Of course I do!"

"Then I guess you'll have to provide what you don't have."

"You sound like Missy. Like I can simply produce a daddy on demand."

"You can. He's standing right here in front of you."

"Nick!" she protested.

But he didn't answer her with words. He wrapped his arms around her and kissed her deeply, longingly, letting her know how much he wanted to be the daddy for the girls—and her husband.

Unfortunately, his actions didn't convince her.

She pushed her way out of his embrace and answered the call from the girls' room that they were ready to be tucked in. She kissed each of them goodnight and Nick followed with a hug.

After closing their bedroom door, Jennifer walked into the living room, with Nick on her heels.

"Jen, I was serious when I offered to be the dad for your little family."

"I can't allow that, Nick. I know our futures will be very different. I won't do something that I know is wrong."

"What are you talking about?" he demanded.

"You are a novelist who is already on Hollywood's radar screen. That's where your future is, Nick. And when it's time for you to go there, I won't be hanging on to your coattails."

"I'm not going to Hollywood, Jen. I'm not a Hollywood-type person. I've told you I'm a homebody. And my home is here with you and the girls."

"Go home, Nick. Maybe your sacrifice won't even be necessary. I'll call Child Services on Monday and make some inquiries."

"You don't understand, Jen. I didn't explain it right. I want to help you keep the girls. But the real reason I'm willing to marry you is because I love you. Period. Nothing more."

"That's very sacrificial of you, Nick. Now, go home."

He pulled her in his arms for one more desperate kiss. She gave in to his embrace, resting in his arms, meeting his lips at every turn, until she finally withdrew.

"Good night, Nick," she whispered, sounding a little like Annie.

He placed his forehead on hers. "We're going to be together, sweetheart. Believe it."

Then he left the apartment.

SATURDAY WAS THE DAY Jennifer had chosen to have Billy and his mother to dinner. She believed it was necessary to become friends with Debra, Billy's mother, if she was to be friends—no, family—with Billy.

Her greatest fear was that Debra might hate her.

She prepared the dinner carefully, but her mind was still debating the issue of the adoption. She hadn't talked to Nick today, and she didn't want to. It was too hard to resist his sweet offer. But she believed it would be the worst thing she could do. She would be holding him back.

However, he would be here for dinner. Hopefully, he wouldn't offer marriage in front of Debra. That would embarrass her.

When there was a knock on her door, she hurried from the kitchen to open it. Much to her relief, it was Billy and his mother. She introduced herself and thanked Debra for allowing Billy to come visit her.

"My dear, I was delighted since you didn't seem like your mother. Your father didn't think we should have anything to do with her."

"He was right, I'm afraid. Come in. Billy, can you introduce the girls to your mother while I finish in the kitchen?"

"Sure. Girls, this is my mom. Mom, this is Steffi. She's six. Annie here is five. And Missy is three, almost four. Right?"

"Right," Steffi said firmly.

"I'm delighted to meet all of you. Billy said you were charming, and he's right."

"Thank you," Steffi said.

Jennifer smiled to herself as she heard the introductions from the kitchen.

When there was another knock on the door, she leaned out of the kitchen. "That should be Nick. Can you get the door, Billy?"

He did as he was asked. "Hi, Nick. Come meet my mom." He made the introductions.

"I'm delighted to meet you, Debra."

"Same here, Nick. Even though you recommended my son work for the FBI."

Jennifer stuck her head out of the kitchen. "I'm glad you know it was Nick who made that suggestion."

Debra laughed. "I'm not worried, Jennifer. Billy's not ready to make a decision like that."

"Oh, good."

"Hi, Jen," Nick said, but she noticed he didn't come any closer to her.

"Hi, Nick. Dinner is almost ready."

When it was, she sat Nick at the opposite end of the

table. And afterward, it was Debra who helped her clear the dishes, not Nick.

Billy leaned close to Nick. "Has something happened? Or is Jennifer not happy with Mom coming?"

"No, it's not your mom. Jennifer is worried about keeping the girls."

"Why?" Billy asked, startled.

Nick explained what happened.

"But you can be the hero and rescue the fair damsels!" Billy exclaimed.

"Jen doesn't seem to feel that way. I've offered, but she told me no."

Billy frowned. "I find that hard to believe. I could've sworn she was in love with you, too. She's always watching you. And you seem to get away with anything you want. I always thought that meant a woman was interested."

"I was hoping, but I guess I was wrong."

"Maybe you've done something that upset her?"

"I don't know what it can be."

NICK REALIZED HE WAS moping around his apartment, wasting time when he should be writing.

But he couldn't help thinking about Jennifer and the girls next door. He was afraid she would lose the girls if she refused to marry him.

But he didn't want her to marry him for just that reason. That wouldn't result in a good marriage. His mother and father had had a good marriage. They had loved each other first and then their children. That was why it had been so sad when his mother had been left a widow.

That was the kind of marriage he wanted. And that was the way he loved Jennifer. He was pretty sure it had been love at first sight, even though he hadn't realized it. Love for Jennifer and the girls.

He wandered into the kitchen and poured himself another cup of coffee. Not that he needed his seventh of the day. But it gave him something to do.

Searching his mind for any other possible way to convince Jennifer of his love, he stared blankly out the window. Nothing came to him. He left the kitchen and wandered to the back windows that opened onto the backyard.

Laughter penetrated the window. He realized Jennifer and the girls were in the backyard with Blondie. He put down his unfinished coffee and headed for the backyard.

ALL THREE LITTLE GIRLS called out his name when Nick came into sight. He found their welcome heartwarming. But he would've liked Jennifer to greet him as warmly.

"Hi, Jen," he said, stopping beside the umbrella-covered chair where she sat, reading.

"Hi, Nick. I'm glad you're still speaking to me."

"Why wouldn't I be?"

"I was afraid I'd hurt your feelings when I said no to your sacrificial offer to marry me."

She gestured to a chair beside her and Nick sat down.

"You didn't hurt my feelings, honey. You broke my heart."

She started to laugh, but the solemn look on his face stopped her. "Really, Nick, if you're honest, you have to know that you have a great future in Hollywood."

"No, I don't know that."

"Then, you'll thank me later."

"No."

"Nick, you're being difficult."

"Hey, Nick, look at me!" Missy called out, hanging upside down on the side bar of the swing set.

"Terrific, Missy, but be careful."

Annie waved to him as she sat in a swing, swaying back and forth, but her feet not leaving the ground.

Steffi sat on top of the slide, trying to get Blondie to climb up the slide to her.

Nick couldn't hold back a smile at the homey sight.

The back door opened and Billy walked out on the deck. "I thought y'all might be out here," he said, crossing over to the table to sit down.

"What are you doing here?" Jennifer asked.

"I just thought I'd drop by. Mom wanted me to bring you this," he said, holding out a white envelope.

Jennifer read it. Then she passed it on to Nick.

Debra had sent a thank-you note for Jennifer's hospitality and expressed how much she'd enjoyed the evening.

"Your mother has great manners," Jennifer said with a smile.

"Yeah, she's great, but it was a nice night. When we first got there, I was afraid you weren't happy about Mom coming. Then Nick explained about the adoption of the girls."

"I'm glad he explained. I don't want you, or your mother, to get the wrong impression. It was…just so unexpected. I went to the exhibit, excited about showing my work, but I didn't expect anyone to want to adopt the girls."

"They are beautiful, Jennifer."

She nodded. "They're even more beautiful inside."

"Like their mom," Nick said softly.

Jennifer turned to him. "Thank you, Nick. That's a lovely compliment."

"It's the truth."

"Nick—" Jennifer began, the tension heavy between them.

"Hi, Billy!" Missy called as she came running up the stairs. "I didn't know you were coming."

Billy held out his arms and Missy jumped into his lap.

The other two girls came running up the stairs. But Annie tripped as she got to the top step and crashed onto the deck, her head hitting hard.

"Annie!" Jennifer screamed as she jumped up to reach her middle child.

But Nick got there first, cradling Annie against his chest.

"Annie, Annie, can you hear me?" Jennifer called, stroking Annie's forehead as her eyes remained closed.

"We need to get Annie to the hospital. Billy, can you stay with the other two?" Nick asked.

Billy assured him he'd stay with them. "I'll take them inside, and you can call as soon as you get word on Annie."

"Right. Ready, Jen?"

"I don't have my purse," she said, and dashed into her apartment for it.

Once she was in the car with her seat belt on, he lowered Annie into her arms. As he did so, Annie blinked several times and stared up at Jennifer.

"Wh-what happened?" she asked.

"You fell and bumped your head, Annie," Jennifer said softly. "How do you feel?"

"My head hurts."

"Okay. Just lie still. We're taking you to the doctor," Jennifer assured her.

Annie closed her eyes again.

"It's good that she woke up, isn't it?" she asked Nick softly.

"Yeah, it's good."

When they got to the hospital, they went to Emergency and Jennifer called Annie's pediatrician. Since his office was nearby, he came to the ER to check Annie out.

Both Nick and Jennifer went into the examining room with Annie.

The doctor said hello to Jennifer. Then he turned to Nick. "And you are?"

"I'm—" He caught himself. He'd almost said he was Annie's father. "I'm a friend."

"I'm sorry but—"

"I want him to stay, Doctor," Jennifer said firmly. "Annie will want him here."

After a look at Nick, the doctor nodded. "All right."

He asked several questions over his shoulder as he examined Annie, in particular how long she was out.

"About a minute or two," Nick said.

"What did she strike her head on?"

"The deck. She tripped on a step and hit her head on it," Jennifer said, her voice trembling.

Nick slid his arm around Jennifer, the first time he'd touched her since her refusal of his offer to marry him.

The doctor talked to Annie as he examined her. "Does your head hurt?"

"Yes."

"Do you remember falling?"

Annie frowned. "Not exactly."

"I see. Were you playing outside?"

"Yes, and we were going upstairs to see Billy. We didn't know he was coming to see us."

"I see. Who is Billy?"

"Mommy said he's our uncle, but I don't know what that means. She didn't meet him until last week, so how can he be our uncle?"

"That's a good question, Annie. Mommy, can you answer Annie's question?"

"Yes, of course. Billy is my half brother, but I hadn't met him until last week. That makes him their uncle."

"I see," the doctor said.

"What do you think, Doctor?"

"I think Annie's got a hard head," he joked, smiling at the girl. Then he turned to Jennifer. "I want to keep her overnight just to be sure."

"Overnight?" Jennifer asked, panic in her voice.

"Yes. You're welcome to stay with her."

"Yes, of course. I—I'll need to make arrangements," she said.

Nick squeezed her shoulder. "Jen, take my car, go home and get what you'll need. Then come back here and I'll go home and take care of Steffi and Missy until you get back home tomorrow."

She stared up at him. "Are you sure, Nick? You won't get any work done and—"

He couldn't stop himself as he bent to kiss her. "Quit worrying about things that don't matter."

"Thank you so much."

"You don't have to thank me," he said roughly. "Just marry me."

Chapter Fifteen

Jennifer flew into the apartment to gather up a clean nightgown for Annie and a change of clothes for herself. Billy and the other two girls followed her around.

"How is Annie?" was Billy's first question.

"Her head hurts but she's okay. The doctor says it's just a precaution to keep her overnight."

"Do you need me to spend the night here?"

"Thanks for offering but Nick's going to stay with the girls. He'll be back in a few minutes after I get to the hospital."

"Yeah, he's great with them. It's too bad you don't love him so he could be their real daddy."

In the process of packing an overnight bag, Jennifer froze, then she stared at him. "What do you mean I don't love him?"

"That's what he told me."

"No, you've got it wrong. I do love him, but—" Her

eyes filled with tears and she called herself ten kinds of fool for letting her heart get broken. "He only offered to help me keep the girls."

"No, Jennifer, he loves you. He told me so that first day I came here. I could see it for myself, but he flat-out told me."

She shook her head and banished the tears. "You don't understand, Billy. He's going to have a life in Hollywood. I'm not raising my children there."

"But he won't have a life there if he doesn't want it." Billy stared at Jennifer, waiting for her response.

"He'll want it. No one can turn down that kind of money."

"He can if he doesn't want to go out there. And Nick doesn't. Didn't he tell you that?"

"Yes, but—" Her head started to pound. There was too much going on inside her brain and she was too worried about Annie to have this talk about Nick. "I can't think about this now. I have to go to Annie."

She hugged the two girls and Billy and ran out the door.

NICK ARRIVED WITH SPECIAL hugs and kisses for the girls.

"Is Annie going to be all right?" Steffi asked, tears in her eyes.

"The doc says she'll be good as new. Mommy will be with her all night. And I'm staying here to take care of you and Missy. Will that be all right?"

Steffi stopped crying immediately.

Missy put it differently. "A'course. You're the daddy!"

"Boy, you rate," Billy said, stepping alongside Nick and giving him a grin.

Nick pulled the girls to him for another quick hug, then he asked them to color a picture for Annie so she'd know they were thinking of her. They ran to their room to do as he'd asked.

"Why didn't I think of that?" Billy asked. "Then they wouldn't have worried themselves to death before you got here."

Nick grinned. "It comes with experience, my man."

Billy paused for a moment. "Experience, huh? Had much experience with women?"

"What do you mean?" Nick gave him a narrow-eyed look.

"You don't seem to be doing too well with my sister." He made sure the girls were out of earshot. "I told Jennifer you love her. But she doesn't believe it."

"I know. She didn't accept it when I told her, either. She thinks I'm only saying it because I want to help her to keep the girls."

"That's not true, is it?"

"No! I've been in love with Jennifer from the first, and the girls, too, but I would love Jennifer with or without them."

Billy smiled broadly and clapped Nick on the back. "Then I suggest you convince her that you don't want to go to Hollywood."

"I've tried."

He thought for a moment, then said, "Maybe if you get an offer, you can turn it down."

"That's already happened."

"Didn't you tell her?"

"No. It didn't seem important at the time." Nick hung his head, annoyed with himself for being so stupid.

"You need that Hollywood guy to tell her."

"Or my agent. I'll arrange that as soon as this crisis is past us."

"That's kind of what she said, too."

Nick shook Billy's hand. "Thanks for trying, Billy."

"Hey, I'm thinking about my sister's happiness."

"Me, too," Nick said with a smile.

JENNIFER DOZED ON THE CHAIR that reclined in Annie's hospital room, but she was up every fifteen minutes to check on Annie. The night seemed interminable; she was never so happy for morning to arrive.

Annie, too, was still a little groggy from lack of sleep.

"I'm too tired to eat breakfast, Mommy," she complained.

"But the doctor may say you can't go home if you don't eat."

Annie's eyes grew big. "Okay. I can eat."

"Good. We'll both eat our breakfasts together."

Though Annie didn't finish all of hers, she ate her eggs and drank her juice. Jennifer got her to eat a couple of bites of bacon.

Afterward as they waited for the doctor, Jennifer

dialed her home number and asked Nick to put the girls on so they could talk to their sister. That phone call cheered Annie up a lot. And Jennifer enjoyed talking to Nick briefly. He was so strong in his beliefs, and he gave her strength.

The doctor gave Annie a clean bill of health and Jennifer called Nick again to come pick them up. He said he and the other two girls would park in front and wait for them to come down.

Annie liked riding down in the wheelchair. Jennifer walked beside her, carrying the overnight bag and holding on to Annie's hand. When they reached the front door, Nick pulled the car right up beside it.

Jennifer helped Annie into the backseat, stuck the overnight bag on the floorboard and slid into the front seat. "Thank you so much for coming to get us, Nick. We were ready to leave, weren't we, Annie?"

"Yes. Thank you, Nick."

"Did they hurt you?" Missy asked.

"No, they were very nice," Annie replied. "But we're pretty tired."

Jennifer concurred. "I think Annie and I will both be glad to take a nap today."

"Steffi, Missy and I voted to pick up hamburgers for lunch so you don't have to prepare anything," Nick interjected. "Is that okay?"

Jennifer smiled wearily at him. "I think that's wonderful, if you don't mind."

"Nope. We voted." He smiled at her. "We're going

to take you both home and let you sleep a little now. Then the other two girls and I will go get lunch."

"Thank you so much, Nick. I don't know how I can repay you."

"It's not necessary."

And that was the last they spoke until he woke her up at noon. The hamburgers were hot and delicious and Jennifer suddenly realized she was hungry. There was very little conversation. After she finished, she smiled sleepily at Nick and left to crawl back into her bed.

Nick put Annie down for her nap and encouraged the other two girls to rest also. Then he read a book in the living room, wanting to make sure that the girls didn't wake Jennifer up until she was rested.

When Jennifer got up a little after four, she found Nick in the kitchen, preparing dinner. "Nick! I can do that."

But Nick steered her out of the kitchen. "You, my dear, have other things to do. Like calling Child Services to find out what will happen about the girls."

"Oh, yes, of course!" She went to the phone in the living room.

Nick never felt time move slower than it did as he waited. He gave Jen her privacy, though he wanted nothing more than to eavesdrop on the phone call. Finally, when fifteen minutes had passed, she rushed into the kitchen and threw her arms around his neck.

"They said I would still get the girls! Even without a husband!"

He kissed her. "I'm so glad."

"You are?"

"Yes. Now, come with me."

To her surprise, he led her back to the phone. He dialed a long-distance number and said, "Jim, I want you to tell the woman who comes on the line about the offer I got to go back to Hollywood and stay until the film is over and what I responded and when." Then he shoved the phone back into Jennifer's hand.

"Hello?"

"Um, I'm not sure who I'm talking to, but—"

"My name is Jennifer. I'm Nick's neighbor."

"I'm Nick's agent, Jim Barnes. When Nick got back from Hollywood, I told him the people out there were very pleased with his work and wanted him to come out there and work until the film is finished."

"They did?"

"Yes, but Nick immediately said no way. He said he was where he wanted to be and if I remember correctly, it had something to do with a special lady, who, I would guess, is you."

Jennifer turned to stare at Nick.

"Well, did he tell you?" Nick asked.

She nodded.

He took the phone from her. "Thanks, Jim." Then he hung it up.

"Did what he said make any difference to you?" he asked Jennifer.

She nodded.

That simple gesture meant so much. It told him Billy had been right. About the proof she needed. About how she felt about him. His own emotion boiled over and came out in a rush.

"Jen, I love you. I don't want to go to Hollywood. I think I can make a good living here, writing my books, not screenplays. But most of all, I want to live my life with you."

"Oh, yes."

"Yes, what, Jen?"

"Yes, I love you."

They smiled and he lowered his head for the kiss he'd been waiting for. Just as their lips met, Missy called urgently from the bedroom. "Mommy?"

Jennifer ran to the girls' bedroom. On the way, she called back, "I think something's burning in the kitchen."

"Damn!" Nick ran for the kitchen.

He never did get that kiss, but something told him life with Jen and the girls would always be this hectic.

He was going to love every minute of it. He would take them all to dinner in any restaurant they could name. It would be his engagement dinner!

NICK LOVED HOLDING Jennifer in his arms. They'd had a great dinner—at a local restaurant, since Nick's meal had burnt—and all through dinner, the ride home and now as they ushered the girls into the living room, he hadn't let her go.

"We have something we want to talk to you about," Nick said to the three towheads.

"Is it bad?" Annie asked.

"No, baby." Jennifer stepped out of his embrace and went to her. "It's real good." She smiled up at Nick. "Nick is going to be your real daddy. We're getting married."

Missy jumped up and down, shouting, "I knew it! I knew it!"

Annie hugged Nick. "I'm so happy you'll be our daddy," she said in her soft voice.

"Me, too, Annie. Me, too."

Steffi hugged him, too. "Now we're a real family. Mommy, Daddy and three children."

"Absolutely," Jennifer said.

"So when will Daddy move in with us?" Missy asked.

Nick couldn't answer that. He looked at Jennifer. "I don't know."

"Whenever he wants," Jennifer said. The three little girls cheered and hugged them again.

"So, you'll be here when we wake up in the morning, and I can call you Daddy?" Missy asked.

Nick swung her into his lap. "Yes, yes, and yes again."

"What are all those yeses for?" Annie asked.

"For all the times Missy is going to ask again," Nick said with a grin. "We're all going to be a family forever. You'll never get away from us," he said, pretending to scare them.

But that didn't fool them. They just piled on him again, giggling.

The girls were so excited, it seemed to take forever to settle them into bed.

When they did, he asked Missy's question again. "When do I move in here, the future Mrs. Barry?"

"Mmm, how about tonight?"

"Jen, are you sure? I don't mind waiting. We're going to have the rest of our lives together, so I can wait until you're ready."

"I know. But I'm ready. We can go get our license tomorrow and be married in three days. But a piece of paper doesn't make a marriage, Nick."

"I love you so much, Jennifer," he said, scooping her up into his arms and heading down the hall to her room. He carried her to the bed. Then he looked around. "I think we may have to make some changes in here."

Jennifer sat up. "Oh, really? What do you want changed?"

"I don't think peach is the right color for *our* bedroom."

"Well, you could be right, but I was wondering if we should look for a house."

"You want to move?"

"Why not? We could rent out both our apartments and make more than enough for a house payment."

"Sweetheart, we'd have to own them to make money."

"Sweetheart, we do own them."

Nick gave her a puzzled look. "What are you talking about?"

"I forgot you didn't know. I'm your landlord."

"You own the fourplex? My, your grandmother was very generous to you."

"More than you know. I own all four fourplexes on this street."

"You what?"

"My grandmother bought the land and had the four-plexes built to provide income for her and then for me, when she left them to me."

"But, Jennifer, I don't think I can match that kind of money, at least not for more than a year or two."

Jennifer laughed. "I'm impressed that you could match it for a year or two, Nick."

"Let's talk about this tomorrow when I can concentrate on it, sweetheart. My mind is focused on you right now." He leaned down to her. "Are you still sure you want to share your bed with me tonight?"

"I'm sure," she said, and held her arms out to him. He joined her on the bed and kissed her, this time giving her the kiss he'd dreamed of.

When he slipped his hand beneath her shirt, he paused again. "Still sure, sweetheart?"

"I'm so sure, I'm going to help you," she said, removing her blouse. Then she reached out for his shirt. "Are you sure?" she teased.

"Hell, yes." After that, they disrobed quickly, but Nick kept his eyes on Jennifer. He loved the freedom with which she moved.

When she started removing her bra, he stopped

her. "Let me. I've had dreams about this. I don't just want to watch."

"All right," Jennifer agreed with a smile. When he reached for her bra, she reached for his jeans.

"Hey lady, what are you doing?"

"I've had a few dreams of my own," she told him, not stopping. "Aha! Boxers!"

"All you had to do was ask," he said with a grin. "I have no secrets. Not anymore."

"I guess I could've asked Mrs. Carroll, but finding out this way is more fun."

"I couldn't agree more," he said softly as he cupped her bare breasts. He dropped a kiss on each breast and then pulled her to him and kissed her again. "Jen, I love you so much."

"Even more than the women in Hollywood?"

"They couldn't even compare to you. They're fool's gold, Jen. You're twenty-four karat. Tomorrow, we're going to find you a ring. In fact, we'll get both of us a ring. I want everyone to know that I'm taken."

"Me, too, but you seem to be a little distracted. Have you forgotten what we're doing?"

He laughed. "No, I haven't forgotten, sweetheart." He kissed her again while he removed the rest of her clothes as well as his. Then he suddenly stopped. "Do you have a lock on your bedroom door?"

"No, but I've taught the girls to knock before—"

"What's that?" Nick gasped, rising up.

"Nick, it's the sprinkler system. It comes on every night. The girls are sound sleepers, I promise."

"Okay, but when we look for a house, we need a door with a lock on it. I don't want to have to explain the facts of life to the girls just yet."

Jennifer laughed. "I'm sure you'd do a great job of it."

Nick shuddered. "Maybe, in a few years, but I'd prefer to discuss the facts of life with you—tonight."

Jennifer wrapped her arms around his neck. "I'm a quick learner, Mr. Barry, I promise."

He smiled at her. "Oh, I believe you, the future Mrs. Barry." Then he buried himself in her welcoming warmth.

AFTERWARD AS SHE LAY in his arms, Jennifer said, "Do you realize we forgot to use a condom?"

"Yeah, but I promise I'm safe. I don't have any diseases."

She laughed. "That's not what I was worried about."

"It's not?"

"No. I'm not on any birth control."

"Oh. I hadn't thought of that. Is that a problem for you?"

"Not for me, if you can handle *four* children."

Nick grinned. "What's one more? And maybe we could have a boy this time."

"This time? You forget I didn't give birth the other three times?"

"No, but I think they're your daughters in your heart, even if they aren't your daughters by birth."

She cradled his jaw in her hand, looking into his eyes and seeing his love for her and the girls. She'd taken in the girls to give them a loving home and somehow she'd found a man to give her the family she'd always wanted. How had she ever gotten so lucky to find Nick? She may never know, but she'd spend a lifetime reveling in their happiness.

She smiled at him. "They're your daughters, too. After all, Missy claimed you that first day."

"Yeah. That was the luckiest day of my life."

"For me, too, Nick. For me, too."

* * * * *

*Watch for Judy Christenberry's next book
in the* DALLAS DUETS *series,*
THE MARRYING KIND,
*coming May 2007, only from
Harlequin American Romance!*

Happily ever after is just the beginning...

Turn the page for a sneak preview of
DANCING ON SUNDAY AFTERNOONS
by
Linda Cardillo

Harlequin Everlasting—
Every great love has a story to tell.™
A brand-new line from Harlequin Books
launching this February!

Prologue

Giulia D'Orazio
1983

I had two husbands—Paolo and Salvatore.

Salvatore and I were married for thirty-two years. I still live in the house he bought for us; I still sleep in our bed. All around me are the signs of our life together. My bedroom window looks out over the garden he planted. In the middle of the city, he coaxed tomatoes, peppers, zucchini—even grapes for his wine—out of the ground. On weekends, he used to drive up to his cousin's farm in Waterbury and bring back manure. In the winter, he wrapped the peach tree and the fig tree with rags and black rubber hoses against the cold, his massive, coarse hands gentling those trees as if they were his fragile-skinned babies. My neighbor, Dominic Grazza, does that for me now. My boys have no time for the garden.

In the front of the house, Salvatore planted roses. The roses I take care of myself. They are giant, cream-colored, fragrant. In the afternoons, I like to sit out on the porch with my coffee, protected from the eyes of the neighborhood by that curtain of flowers.

Salvatore died in this house thirty-five years ago. In the last months, he lay on the sofa in the parlor so he could be in the middle of everything. Except for the two oldest boys, all the children were still at home and we ate together every evening. Salvatore could see the dining room table from the sofa, and he could hear everything that was said. "I'm not dead, yet," he told me. "I want to know what's going on."

When my first grandchild, Cara, was born, we brought her to him, and he held her on his chest, stroking her tiny head. Sometimes they fell asleep together.

Over on the radiator cover in the corner of the parlor is the portrait Salvatore and I had taken on our twenty-fifth anniversary. This brooch I'm wearing today, with the diamonds—I'm wearing it in the photograph also—Salvatore gave it to me that day. Upstairs on my dresser is a jewelry box filled with necklaces and bracelets and earrings. All from Salvatore.

I am surrounded by the things Salvatore gave me, or

did for me. But, God forgive me, as I lie alone now in my bed, it is Paolo I remember.

Paolo left me nothing. Nothing, that is, that my family, especially my sisters, thought had any value. No house. No diamonds. Not even a photograph.

But after he was gone, and I could catch my breath from the pain, I knew that I still had something. In the middle of the night, I sat alone and held them in my hands, reading the words over and over until I heard his voice in my head. I had Paolo's letters.

* * * * *

Be sure to look for
DANCING ON SUNDAY AFTERNOONS
available January 30, 2007.
And look, too, for our other
Everlasting title available,
FALL FROM GRACE
by Kristi Gold.

FALL FROM GRACE
is a deeply emotional story of
what a long-term love really means.
As Jack and Anne Morgan discover,
marriage vows can be broken—but
they can be mended, too.
And the memories of their marriage have
an unexpected power to bring back
a love that never really left....

HARLEQUIN® *Romance*®

What a month!

In February watch for

Rancher and Protector
Part of the Western Weddings miniseries
BY JUDY CHRISTENBERRY

The Boss's Pregnancy Proposal
BY RAYE MORGAN

Also in February, expect
MORE of what you love
as the Harlequin Romance line
increases to six titles per month.

This February...

Catch NASCAR Superstar **Carl Edwards** *in*

SPEED DATING!

Kendall assesses risk for a living—
so she's the last person you'd
expect to see on the arm of a
race-car driver who thrives on the
unpredictable. But when a bizarre
turn of events—and NASCAR
hotshot Dylan Hargreave—inspire
her to trade in her ever-so-structured
existence for "life in the fast lane"
she starts to feel she might be
on to something!

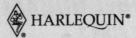

HARLEQUIN®

American **ROMANCE®**

COMING NEXT MONTH

#1149 THE DOCTOR'S LITTLE SECRET by Jacqueline Diamond
Fatherhood
Dr. Russ McKenzie doesn't have much in common with shoot-from-the-hip policewoman Rachel Byers. Nevertheless, he shares his little secret with her. Soon the two of them could be keeping it for life!

#1150 HER PERFECT HERO by Kara Lennox
Firehouse 59
The firefighters of Firehouse 59 are stunned when Julie Polk decides to convert a local hangout into a *tearoom!* Determined not to let that happen, they elect resident Casanova Tony Veracruz to sweet-talk the blonde into changing her mind. But when Tony wants more than just a fling with Julie, he's not sure where his loyalties lie....

#1151 ONCE A COWBOY by Linda Warren
Brodie Hayes is a former rodeo star, now a rancher—a cowboy through and through. Yet when he finds out some shocking news about the circumstances of his birth, he begins to question his identity. Luckily, private investigator Alexandra Donovan is there to help him find the truth—but will it really change who he is?

#1152 THE SHERIFF'S SECOND CHANCE by Leandra Logan
When Ethan Taggert, sheriff of Maple Junction, Wisconsin, hears Kelsey Graham is coming home for the first time in ten years, he wants to be there when she arrives. Not only is he eagerly anticipating seeing his former crush, he's also there to protect her. After all, there's a reason she couldn't return home before now....

www.eHarlequin.com

HARCNM0107